"Groundbreaking and unique, character-driven crime fiction written in my favourite dialect. I was mesmerized." —Deon Meyer

"A searing crime novel, a spellbinding story of queer desire, friendship, and resilience, and a trailblazing work of fiction, *Innie Shadows* is an authentic, unsentimental, fearless achievement. Even in its darkest moments, it brims with life." —Kathy Friedman, author of *All the Shining People*

"Deftly interweaving broader themes of colonization and queerness, *Innie Shadows* is a fast-paced yet richly detailed story set in a Cape Town neighbourhood struggling with addiction and violence. The characters leap off the page, fully human, as Olivia M. Coetzee urges the reader to consider the powers of love and belief, and all the places they may lead us." —Adriana Chartrand, author of *An Ordinary Violence*

"Olivia M. Coetzee's swift-moving, tautly constructed novel about the inhabitants of the Shadows is suspenseful, surprising, and, in the end, devastating." —Méira Cook, author of *The Full Catastrophe*

"Fresh, searing, gritty, richly vivid, and fearless, *Innie Shadows* is not afraid to speak its truth. *Innie Shadows*

will take you deep into a world ruled by desire, greed, lust, and the raw destruction of all that is vulnerable, precious, and innocent. But there is love, hope, joy, and rebirth. As a character in the book says, 'And you say there's nothing beautiful here.' There most certainly is."
—Lisa de Nikolits, author of *Everything You Dream is Real*, *Rotten Peaches*, and *The Witchdoctor's Bones*

"Olivia M. Coetzee crafts a new language to bring to life stories of dispossession from those left behind in the transition to democracy. This haunting novel will stay with the reader long after the final page is turned."
—Barbara Boswell, author of *And Wrote My Story Anyway: Black South African Women Novels as Feminism*

"Olivia M. Coetzee writes Cape Town as it lies on the tongue of her speakers." —Herschelle Benjamin, LitNet

INNIE SHADOWS

OLIVIA M. COETZEE

SPIDERLINE

First published as *Innie Shadows* in Kaaps in 2019 by Modjaji Books
First published in English in 2024 by House of Anansi Press Inc.
houseofanansi.com

House of Anansi Press is committed to protecting our natural environment.
This book is made of material from well-managed FSC®-certified forests, recycled
materials, and other controlled sources.

House of Anansi Press is a Global Certified Accessible™ (GCA by Benetech) publisher.
The ebook version of this book meets stringent accessibility standards and is available
to readers with print disabilities.

28 27 26 25 24   1 2 3 4 5

Library and Archives Canada Cataloguing in Publication
Title: Innie shadows / Olivia M. Coetzee.
Other titles: Innie shadows. English
Names: Coetzee, Olivia M., author, translator.
Description: Author is also the translator. | Translation of: Innie shadows. |
Translated from the Kaaps.
Identifiers: Canadiana (print) 20240353722 | Canadiana (ebook) 20240357361 |
ISBN 9781487012526 (softcover) | ISBN 9781487012533 (EPUB)
Subjects: LCGFT: Detective and mystery fiction. | LCGFT: Novels.
Classification: LCC PT6593.13.O38 I5613 2024 | DDC 839.3/636—dc23

Cover text and artwork: Rudi de Wet

*House of Anansi Press is grateful for the privilege to work on and create from the Traditional
Territory of many Nations, including the Anishinabeg, the Wendat, and the Haudenosaunee,
as well as the Treaty Lands of the Mississaugas of the Credit.*

*We acknowledge for their financial support of our publishing program the Canada Council for
the Arts, the Ontario Arts Council, and the Government of Canada.*

*Publication of this work has been made possible with the financial support
from the PEN Afrikaans Translation Fund.*

Printed and bound in Canada

To my ancestors.

I couldn't walk this path without your love, trust, protection, and guidance.

This novel contains depictions of drug use,
rape, homophobia, and violence.
Take care when reading.

1

WHERE'S CARL?

Monday

I t was a dark and cloudy Monday morning. Veronique Plaatjies, or Nique, as her family and friends knew her, sat at her makeshift desk. She started every morning the same way. A steaming cup of black coffee, pen in hand, her journal in front of her, the curtains pulled back and windows pushed slightly open: a perfect frame for watching the world go by. A few old magazines were stacked on a corner of Nique's desk. Receipts and bills lay scattered next to an empty handbag. She tucked one end of the towel wrapped around her body back into place, leaned back into the chair, and reached for her coffee mug. Her eyes jumped over the potted plants and the small herb garden that she had started in the corner of her yard. She never thought she would have a house to call her own, let alone a garden. But there were many things she never thought she would accomplish.

She opened the journal her boyfriend, Byron, had bought her to celebrate their seventh year together. Everyone called him the Don of the Shadows because it didn't matter what happened in the Shadows, Byron knew about it. He was the boss of it all.

Winter is here, she wrote. Her head was cluttered with worries. Gershwin and his constant troubles with his mother. Carl, who she had last seen a week ago. Sometimes Nique wished she could go and pack Gershwin's bags herself, but she knew life didn't work like that. She scribbled across the page: *Toxic relationships last because people stay. People will do what they think they must do, even if it means staying in places where they're not wanted.* But she never understood straight people's obsession with trying to fix those who didn't love like they did. What was there to fix? And Gershwin's mother, Rose, seemed to be the captain of that club. If she only knew that her son was secretly dating her crush, Pastor Richard. But Nique would rather deal with Gershwin's demons than the dragon devouring Carl. She accepted that Carl was a lost cause. Meth addiction was an illness with no cure, and no one was to blame for the life choices he had made. Aunty Merle always said, "We make choices, and those choices pave the way for us."

Nique's focus floated to the street. Most mornings she made up stories about the people she saw outside her window, but today she just sat and watched them pass by. She was struggling to calm the uneasy feeling in the pit of her stomach. The rhythmic flow of people moved in and out of her window frame. Little kids dressed in oversized hand-me-downs and backpacks too big for their bodies chased after their older siblings who rushed down the street to catch either a bus or a train to school. A small group of women walked into the frame, all with handbags tucked under their arms as they shouldered against the wind. All of them in a hurry to board a crowded bus that would take them into the city, where they'd spend the day working at one of the last remaining clothing factories. Nique smiled as she saw a few of her customers walk by. It didn't matter how many times she did their hair over the weekend, come Monday, their curls would be tucked away under their colourful headscarves. The women exploded in laughter as they exited Nique's window frame. Next came a group of workers dressed in paint-stained blue overalls. They were listening to loud music playing over a boom box hidden out of sight in a backpack.

When Nique had stayed in Joburg the previous year, she had often longed for the rhythmic flow of the Shadows. She had missed the comforting familiarity of everyday life. Nique's eyes zoomed in on her neighbours, two elderly sisters, as they shuffled through their front gate, waving down a minibus taxi coming up the street.

Nique took a sip of her coffee, which had lost its heat and sweetness. She sighed with satisfaction because that's how she liked her coffee: cold, bitter, and with no cream. Her friends never understood her love for cold coffee.

They also never understood her taste in men. The men were either ugly, dark-skinned, or fat, or in Byron's case, all three. But she found comfort in Byron, and what others saw as ugly and unattractive she saw as supportive and loving. The fact that he was the biggest gangster in the Shadows didn't matter to her, nor did his wife or kids. It was love at first sight, and he never once disrespected Nique for the way her body had been before her operations.

A seagull caught Nique's eye, fighting the merciless winds beneath the thick cloudy skies in the direction of Table Mountain. It pushed forward, then was thrown back, then pushed forward again. The bird's flight continued for a few minutes before it suddenly dropped down, probably tired of struggling to get where it needed to go. The seagull landed somewhere outside Nique's view. She always wondered if other people also saw Table Mountain as a landmark to show where home was. If they saw what she saw—that the unmistakable sight of Table Mountain meant she was home.

The alarm on her cellphone rang out. Nique got up to silence it and unplugged the cellphone from its charger. The faint smell of perfume that wafted from the jersey she had flung over the chair next to her bed reminded her of her mother. Nique thought back to the last few weeks before her mother passed. The house had been full of people she didn't know: her mother's work colleagues and well-meaning neighbours who fussed around her mother's bed. They all wanted to be there for Aunty

Sandy but ignored Nique like dust on the mantelpiece. Some walked around her; others looked at the wall or a crack in the cement floor while talking to her. Nique's mother had refused to accept her son as a woman, and the neighbours didn't make it any easier for her mom to accept Nique as a trans woman.

Nique's attention returned to her front gate where a minibus taxi was stopped. Music boomed, shaking the taxi. She felt sorry for people who had to ride in taxis like that, music blasting out of the speakers no matter the time of day or night. Her neighbours shouted at the driver as the taxi's sliding door closed and it moved off without them. Two more women joined them as they waited for the next taxi that came down the street. This time Nique heard no music. They slipped into the taxi, disappearing one by one.

She sat back down at her desk and her pen scribbled across the page. Every day it was the same story. The same people, with the same problems, walking in the footsteps of the day before. *The Shadows: A TV Drama*, she thought. But she loved its drama. The small houses were squashed in next to each other, with asbestos-cement roofs that shimmered green and gold when the sun rose, each one standing at attention before Table Mountain. Sometimes she prayed to win the lottery so she could help her people living in poverty. But no matter how bare people's cupboards were, they always made it a point to paint their houses with bright colours and decorate their gardens with colourful flowers and green shrubs, shining a light into the dark corners of their lives in the Shadows.

Nique picked up her coffee mug and rubbed her hand over the big red letters on the white porcelain. BESTIES, they read. She remembered the day she got it, a few months before she left for Joburg. The five of them— Gershwin, Sara, Ley, Carl, and Nique—had gone out to celebrate Carl's birthday. They'd been inseparable since primary school, their bond only growing stronger as they got older. "The Terrible Five," Aunty Merle always called them. Nique wanted matching necklaces, but Sara reminded her of the time she was walking around with a green neck from the cheap necklace she had bought at the outdoor market that popped up at the Grand Parade market in front of City Hall every Wednesday and Saturday. That was the last year they really knew Carl, before he started hanging with the wrong crowd, drinking and drugging. No one could have imagined that Carl would be the one to get lost in the Shadows.

Nique thought back to the first couple of months after Carl lost his mother, how they had intervention after intervention to try to get him through his pain and away from the meth pipe. It was painful for them to see an honour student fall into the cracks created by his mother's illness, dropping out of school, losing his way with his meth buddies. Carl's sister, Mandy, blamed him for his mother's death. As if anyone was to blame for the big C. Nique tried to get Carl to talk about his loss, but her mother always told her, you can only do so much for someone else until you lose yourself. Nique invited him to live with her, but she knew that the Carl she had grown up with and held dear in her heart was long gone. The new Carl would never stay for long before the dragon inside him needed to feed. Nique knew how difficult it was for people struggling with meth. Like one of her neighbours who lost more than just the things in her home because her two teenage kids started breaking down their house one brick at a time to get money for their next fix.

The first time Carl stole from her, he took her toaster and kettle. As usual when she got home at night, she first went to her bedroom to get undressed, and then to the kitchen to make herself a cup of coffee before sitting on the porch. But when she entered the kitchen, the kettle was missing. Her first instinct was to call the cops, but after a quick walk-through of her house she determined no windows or doors had been broken into. That's when she knew that the only person who could be to blame was Carl. He was her friend, so she would rather hand him over to the cops than to Byron and his boys, who would do more than just rough him up. But calling the cops was a waste of time; they rarely showed up in the Shadows.

She had called Carl to confront him but remembered that he sold every phone he had, even the ones she gave him. Carl's backpack and the set of clothes she had hung up in the cupboard in her guest room for him were gone. She had to accept that Carl had finally stolen from her. Still, she couldn't help fighting with herself, not wanting to believe that everything people were saying about Carl was true.

Nique didn't see or speak to Carl for a month after that. She was angry, but she hoped that Carl had a good explanation. She hoped that it was all just a big mistake, but a voice in her head kept reminding her that she was holding on to false hope. Byron scolded her for allowing Carl to stay with her. He didn't want to hear about how she needed to help him and offered to fix her problem, but Nique didn't want to hear anything about it. She swore to Byron that she would never allow Carl back in her life. She knew she couldn't allow Carl back because she knew she couldn't go through him stealing from her again. But in her heart she knew, too, that she could never turn Carl away. She knew Carl's routine. She would come home after work and find her house dark, with no sign of life. She would then know it was time to take stock of her belongings. She always started with the hole she'd made in her bed where she hid her dead mother's jewellery; the only photo she had of her and her mother, the one where she was forced to dress in a suit for her confirmation; and a few hundred-rand notes she kept for emergencies. She knew Carl knew about her secret stash, but he never stole the money. Maybe there was still a piece of him hiding from the dragon. It seemed like that last piece fought back when he was with her.

Those times she allowed him to come back and stay with her, small items would disappear, like a few packs of cigarettes from the carton she kept in her bedroom cupboard, hairbrushes, or sealed bottles of detergent. She always let him back, in and he always did the same thing, and proved Byron right. Maybe her mother had a point when she said Nique would eventually lose herself trying to help others.

Nique shifted in her chair, her thoughts still on Carl. He made sure to always show up when she asked him to. The last time she saw him was when she went on her weekly visit to Byron's. It was the same Sunday night she saw Gershwin's mother, Rose, rushing out of the gambling room at Byron's Shebeen. Nique was shocked to see a deacon of the local church storming out of a gambling room. Byron's bouncers always had stories to tell about a customer named Rose, but Nique had never thought it could be the Rose she knew who went around cursing sinners like her son and his gay friends. Everyone was the devil in Rose's eyes, but Nique could see the darkness that Rose carried around inside her. Abusive behaviour comes from being abused, Nique told herself when Gershwin complained about his mother's episodes. Gershwin was another friend who she'd never turn away. If only he could stand up to his mother's constant abuse to escape the prison he lived in. Nique sighed. Maybe Gershwin would finally leave if he found out about his mother's secret life.

Nique drew little hearts in every corner of the page in front of her. Her tummy moaned. She checked the time on her cell. "Eight a.m.," she said, as her tummy groaned again. "No wonder you're putting on such a big show."

Her cellphone vibrated with an email notification. Nique scraped her chair against the cement floor she had painted white after her mother's passing, walked over to her closet, and pulled on its handles. The doors swung open with a slight squeak from the hinges. She moved the hangers from one side to the other as she decided on her outfit for the day. Nique caught her full-body reflection in the mirror hanging on the inside of one of the closet doors. She moved closer, smoothing her perfectly plucked eyebrows. She didn't believe in putting on too much makeup but loved painting her lips bright red when she visited Byron every Sunday. Nique dropped her towel to her feet and stared at her perfect body. She was finally the woman she had wanted to be all her life. She moved her hands over her firm breasts. Byron had wanted to know why she had to go for the operations when she had been perfect to him the way she was, but then he couldn't keep his hands off her after her body healed. It didn't matter to her that her friends didn't understand why she chose to have her surgeries because living her true self was all that mattered to her. She had only been disappointed in Gershwin and Ley, thinking they would have understood her choices because they knew how hard it was to live life under the rainbow umbrella. But Gershwin had finally come to accept her, and over time the rest of her friends did, too.

Nique pulled on a pair of bikini panties, followed by tight-fitting white track pants. She pushed her feet back into her pink slippers without putting on socks. Nique put on an oversized T-shirt without a bra and topped off her outfit with a bright yellow hoodie. She returned to her makeshift desk and noticed raindrops on the windowpanes. Coffee mug in hand, she wandered back into the kitchen. Sometimes she missed having family around, but living alone came with privileges. The fewer people who knew about what was going on in your life, the better.

Nique was distracted by a knock at her front door. "Who's there?" she shouted from the kitchen. "Coming!" Nique shouted at the second knock that was a few decibels louder than the first.

"Hi, Ley!" Nique smiled at the young detective standing at her front door. "I thought you forgot where I live." She had last seen her cousin Johnley Sanders the year before at Johnley's mother's sixtieth birthday party, where too much alcohol and family drama led to Ley being outed to her mother and the rest of the community.

Ley forced a smile and rubbed her sunburned nose as she followed Nique into the living room. She remembered her mother's sixtieth too well. Everyone had too much to drink in too short a time. Ley had gotten angry because of Carl's constant flirting with Nique in front of the church people at the party. Nique had told her to concern herself with what was happening in her own life and not with what others were doing. Then Nique had asked Ley about the woman she was living with. Ley remembered the way her mother's expression went from confusion to shock. Her mother made excuses to the pastor and his congregation when Ley didn't say anything to defend herself to let her know that Nique was just joking. But Nique wasn't joking. And Ley couldn't calm the worry in her mother's voice when she asked what Nique was talking about. *How do you tell your staunch Christian mother that the person you love is not the one she wants for you?* Ley thought, remembering her mother's sixtieth birthday party.

Yeah, and you think people don't know that you're playing for the other team, Nique thought, as her eyes jumped over her cousin's fitted men's shirt, boy's haircut, Levi jeans, and work boots.

"Yes, Vern, is something wrong?" Ley asked. She recognized the judging stare people always gave her when they saw how she dressed in men's clothes.

"It's Nique now," Nique said. "And no, you know I love your wardrobe." Nique pulled a cigarette from the pack on the coffee table. "How's your mom?" she asked, and took a drag, thinking about how many people still called her by the name her mother gave her. It had taken her a while to change her name because she wanted something close to her grandfather's name: Vernon Plaatjies. Veronique felt like the right name to pick.

"She's just her usual self," Ley said. "But why are you asking me when you live a few streets from her?"

"When are we meeting your fiancée?" Nique asked, ignoring Ley's question. "You don't have to hide her from us."

"Nobody is hiding anything, but that's not why I'm here," Ley said. "I'm sorry to just pop in without calling—well, I tried, but your number goes straight to voice mail."

"What do you mean, it goes straight to voice mail? You sure you dialed the right number? Because Carl stole one of my phones, too." Nique flicked the ash from her cigarette and bent down to pick up the pack she could see sticking out below the small coffee table next to the couch. She opened it and remembered it was the empty packet she had been looking for the night before.

"You need another smoke?" Ley asked. She pulled a pack of Marlboros from her jeans pocket and threw a cigarette onto the coffee table.

"Thanks, but those are a bit too strong for me," said Nique.

"When did Carl steal your phone?"

"Well, he needed a place to stay after his sister's boy-friend gave him a hiding. He arrived here with bruised ribs and a black eye, but his injuries didn't stop him from stealing the phone and leaving after two days," said Nique. "I'm glad he took the burner instead of my contract phone. I guess that's why you couldn't reach me. It's weird that the number is still active."

"Why did you allow him to come back?" asked Ley.

"He probably couldn't sell the phone. It serves him right," Nique said, ignoring Ley's question again. She knew good and well that she'd always allow Carl to come back. "It will teach him to fucking leave people's shit alone."

"Why didn't you call the cops?" asked Ley.

"What exactly would the cops have done? I mean, he was here, and then he was gone, and the phone left with him. The next time I saw him was at Byron's Shebeen. And you know what happens there. I thought I did something right by giving him a place to stay," Nique said. "And besides, can you imagine the cops trying to locate a burner in the Shadows?" They laughed at Nique's attempt at a joke.

Nique walked over to the front door and pulled it slightly ajar to allow Ley's smoke to filter out and some fresh air in. "You know about Byron's place, right?" asked Nique.

"Who doesn't?" said Ley.

"Have you been there yet?"

"Haven't been there. Does Carl normally hang out there?"

"Yes, that's where we always see each other," said Nique.

"So you know he's missing then?"

"Missing?" Nique asked. "Carl's not missing. Who told you that?" Nique slumped back onto the couch and curled her legs up next to her. "He's changed a lot since he started with that shit. He normally disappears but pops up after a week or so. It's nothing new."

Ley pulled out another cigarette from her packet lying on the coffee table. She settled into the smoke. "How do you know about Carl disappearing from time to time?

"Byron and his guards ask me where Carl is when he stops coming to the shebeen," said Nique. Ley's eyes burning into her back, she walked over to the living room window and flung it open to try to hide the heat flushing her cheeks. "Is that your car?" she asked, attempting to dodge a follow-up question from Ley about her frequenting Byron's Shebeen. Nique knew she couldn't lie to her cousin, and she preferred to keep her relationship with Bryon just between the two of them.

"Nope, that's one of the perks of the job," Ley said as she put out her cigarette in the ashtray. "After they promoted me to detective, they gave me the car to use."

"Wow, that's nice," said Nique with a smile. "Congrats on the job and your new car."

"Yeah, thanks. But it's nothing to write home about," said Ley. "It's the same story every day. You won't believe the things people do out there. Sometimes I'm not sure if it's all worth the pay."

"Of course I can believe the bullshit," said Nique. "Or did you forget where I live?"

"You know, Carl's sister has been on my case for the past couple of days, calling me more than she should," Ley said. "She told me she hasn't seen Carl for nearly three weeks."

"How did she get your number?"

"I don't know," said Ley. "But I wouldn't be surprised if my mother gave it to her."

"I don't think your mother would speak to her. You know how she feels about people who drink," said Nique. "Three weeks? I'm sure Carl's sister has probably just been looking down the bottle too much. That's why she can't find him."

"She's probably just worried," said Ley. "Apparently, he didn't bring her any money for food."

"Mm, just as I thought. She's looking for money," said Nique. "Now she's making up stories that he's missing, and you fell for her sob stories. I saw Carl last week at Byron's Shebeen. His sister needs help. The bottle isn't doing her any good."

"She told me that social services visited her a few weeks back and took her kids," Ley said and took a drag from a new cigarette.

"I don't understand why she can't give up the bottle. I mean, if anything, she should think of her kids. And besides, Ley, since when do you believe the shit a drunk person tells you? Carl isn't missing. I'm sure he's just with Toothless again."

"But you know what they say, a drunk person always tells the truth," said Ley. "Which one is Toothless? All the druggies are starting to look the same out here."

"You remember the hundred-metre sprints in high school?" asked Nique. "You remember the brothers we always cheered for? They live over on Hope Street. Well, Toothless is one of them. He got his nickname after the meth did a number on him. He lost most of his teeth and his hair fell out in weird places. He also walked off with almost everything in his grandma's house. Toothless's brother almost killed him the last time he tried to steal from them."

"Oh, yes, the Dixon brothers, right?" asked Ley.

Nique whacked at a fly buzzing around her head. "You would think it's an invitation to a flies-only party when you open the windows, even with this rainy weather," she said. "Yeah, the famous Dixon brothers."

"Who could've imagined they would go down like

this?" said Ley. "It just shows you nothing is written in stone."

"It's true," said Nique. "No one could've predicted that Carl and Toothless, our star students, would turn out like this. Meth doesn't ask for permission. It just takes what it wants."

They both sat in silence for a bit, each in their own world. Ley played with an unlit cigarette. She held it up to her nose and inhaled.

"So you're just gonna sniff the thing and not light it?" asked Nique.

"There is nothing better than the smell of a Marlboro," said Ley. "It's calming to the nerves."

"Calming to the nerves?" asked Nique. The two cousins laughed at Nique's confusion. Nique pulled a cigarette from the Marlboro pack and imitated Ley's sniffing. "Now I'm convinced there's something wrong with you," said Nique. "No, ma'am, this stuff smells too strong," she said, and pushed the cigarette back into the packet.

It had been a long time since they had last sat down and laughed together. *Nique looks just like her mom, Aunty Sandy*, Ley thought. The black curls hanging to her shoulders. The light freckles sitting on both sides of her nose. Ley thought back to the day that Aunty Sandy and her only child moved in with them. The child was introduced to her as Vern because her cousin was named after their grandpa. She never understood why Nique always wanted to play the role of mother when they played house in the backyard. But it suited Ley just fine because she always liked playing the dad who took his briefcase in the mornings, left to go and work for his family, and returned home from work to be served by his wife. Ley thought of her blue dress with the puffed shoulders Vern would always pull over his undershirt and briefs, and the oversized high heels Vern would strut in as he pretended to be the ever-faithful wife. Ley's eyes travelled over Nique's breasts. *They look better than mine*, she thought. At last, she saw the woman Nique had become. Ley had refused to see it at her mother's sixtieth birthday party. She had refused to see that Nique was living her truth.

"What's that smile for?" asked Nique. "What are you thinking about?"

"Just thinking about Carl and the last time I saw him," Ley lied. She was too shy to tell her cousin of the past her mind was strolling in. Ley knew that the relationship they had built as kids was dead and buried.

"I know you're worried about Carl, but you'll see, he'll be back," Nique said unconvincingly. "It's just that the last time I saw him, he was high on meth and didn't want to talk to me."

"I know there's something really wrong," said Ley. "I can feel it."

"Go and look for him at Byron's," said Nique. "I'm sure they'll have some information of his whereabouts." She tapped her nails on her cellphone's screen. "Yeah, something felt off the last time I saw him, but maybe I'm just looking for things that weren't there."

"You know, when someone is as persistent as his sister's

been about him being gone, then we have to listen," said Ley. "We live in a dirty world. I see things daily that would drive anyone insane. It's not easy, this job. The other day I had a case where a police officer caught his wife cheating on him with his best friend. He then told himself that their child was not his. He pulled out his gun and shot the child, then his wife. Finally, he turned the gun on himself."

"The motherfucker," said Nique.

"Yeah, he is. The gun jammed when he tried to shoot himself. He tried running, but was caught. Now he's in Pollsmoor among the men he put there," said Ley.

"It serves him right. I'm sure he thought he'd get away with it," said Nique. "It's really shocking, the world we're living in." She stood up and walked to the front door to get some fresh air. "It's like a hotbox in here." She laughed, waving at the cigarette smoke hanging in the air. She stepped out onto her porch.

"I'll ask around about Carl," said Ley as she followed Nique out onto the porch. "Someone must've seen him. And I'll visit the shebeen." She coughed to clear her scratchy throat. "Can I please get some water?"

"I'm sorry. You've been here for a while, and I haven't offered you anything to drink. Would you like some coffee or tea?" asked Nique.

"No, don't worry, water is all I need now," said Ley, as Nique stepped back into the house. "I have to leave soon anyway. There's still a lot to do."

Nique's footsteps disappeared into the kitchen. The cupboard door's hinges creaked as she got a glass. Nique turned on the tap full blast. She shrieked as water squirted her face, and she rushed to close the tap. She grabbed a clean dish towel to dry the water off.

"Are you okay?" Ley asked.

"Yes, I am," Nique said, as she walked back into the living room, a few drops of water still dripping from her chin. "Opened the tap too wide," she said.

"Thanks," said Ley, as she took the glass of water and took a long sip.

"Maybe you should ask Toothless first. You'll find him at his friend's house next door to Gershwin's," said Nique. "Do you know about what happened at the rugby field?"

"What happened?" Ley asked, and finished her water.

"I saw a message on one of the WhatsApp chat groups I have on my phone. They found a body this morning. You know how it goes—the streets are already full of people making up stories about who it is. They're saying the body was burned beyond recognition. Apparently, you can't tell if it's a man or a woman. Can you imagine?"

"Well, if it's that bad, then it's gonna take some time to identify the person," said Ley. "I better get going. I told my mother I would visit her before I head back to the office."

"I hope she's doing okay," Nique said. "Tell her I send my love."

"I'll do that. And tell Sara and Gershwin we need to get together soon. Tell them I miss them. And if you hear anything about Carl, or if you see him again, let me know."

"Yes, of course. Mark my words, he's somewhere close by," said Nique, trying to reassure them both. "He knows how to look after himself. But I'll ask my clients and tell the neighbours to let me know if they hear or see anything." Nique watched her cousin get into her white four-door Ford sedan.

Ley's phone vibrated in her jeans pocket. She read the message from her captain summoning her back to the office and threw the cellphone on top of the bunch of files sitting on the passenger seat. Ley looked up and smiled at her cousin waving at her from her front door. She would've told Nique that she'd been at the crime scene, but it was better that no real information get caught in the gossip going around about the body found on the rugby field. Ley turned the key and the car responded with a soft hum. And besides, it would take a while before the DNA results came back from the lab. All they knew was that it was a man in his early twenties. "But that doesn't mean the body is Carl's," she said to herself. Ley honked the car's horn as she drove off.

2

BIG DREAMS AND SAMOSAS

Monday

Sara picked the book up off her lap and pushed it onto the coffee table. Sitting on the couch, she scratched the back of her head and pushed her grey wool beanie to the front of her hair. *Gershwin's gonna be so excited*, she thought. She finally had an opportunity to get out of the Shadows. An opportunity to change and better her life. She opened her journal and traced her finger over the address she had written down. This would be her final interview. She had a feeling the scholarship was hers, but she didn't want to jinx it by telling anyone about it. She knew her dad would have been immensely proud of her, but she was worried about what her mother would say and how she would deal with not seeing her daughter for two years.

Her father had always pushed her, reminding her how important it was to read. Sara paged through the book her father had given her the last night before he died. She thought back to that day. He'd walked in the door that night, book in one hand and backpack in the other. She always asked him if he had nothing else to read than the old book he always carried with him. It was like every chance he got, he had to read a page or two. He always gave the same answer, laughter bubbling up from his happy place. "Nothing better than a book that always teaches you something new about hope and never giving up." He told her that sometimes in life you find a book so full of knowledge that you have to read it again and again and again. He gave her the book, telling her that he hoped it would teach her as it had taught him. She had never understood her father's way of thinking, but his words stayed with her.

"There's always hope because the rain doesn't last forever, Sara."

It was almost like he knew that night would be the last time he would walk through his front door. Even though the stories she found in the book were not Sara's cup of tea, she wished that she could sit with her father one last time.

As Sara slumped over the book on the couch with a grin, her mother, Jennifer, known to everyone as Aunty Jen, walked past the living room, stopped, peeked her head inside, and gazed in silence at her daughter.

"What's that big smile for?" asked Jen.

23

"Just thinking of Daddy," said Sara. "I have a surprise for you."

"So out with it." Jen smiled as she squeezed in next to her daughter on the couch.

"Well." Sara pulled her legs off the couch to make space for her mom. "I applied for a government grant to continue my studies, Mommy. I received an email this morning telling me that I was shortlisted. They called earlier and asked me to come in for a final interview, but something tells me I have it!"

"Wow, my child! I'm so proud of you," said Jen. "This is great news."

"Yes, it is," said Sara. "But there's more, Mommy. No, it's nothing bad," she said quickly when her mom's smile faded.

"You'll give me a heart attack," said Jen. "Just tell me!"

"It's a grant to continue my studies in the States, Mommy. The program—"

"The States? What States are you talking about?"

"America," said Sara.

"America? But how? What about the money? How are you gonna get there? And what about everything they're telling us about the police in America?" asked Jennifer. "My child, the police don't like our kind there."

"Don't worry, Mommy. The grant will cover everything," said Sara. "My plane ticket, my fees, accommodation, and food. Everything. And I'll be safe," Sara tried to convince her mother who was trying to hide the tears trickling down her cheeks.

"What? Are you serious?" Jen said, drying her tears with the bib of her apron.

"Yes," Sara said. "I must go back for my last interview next week."

Jen pulled a tissue out of her pocket and blew her nose loudly. "I don't know what to say, Sara." More tears welled up in Jen's eyes. "What are you gonna wear for your interview? Your father would've been so proud. My own child going off to the United States. My child, I know it's your dream to continue your studies, but I don't want to lose you, too."

"You don't have to worry, Mommy. I'll be safe. Just think about it. This is my ticket out of the Shadows," Sara said. "But I need to do something with my hair." She yanked off her beanie and started pulling at the curls fighting for space on her head.

"You should call Nique to come do your hair," said Jen.

"Yes, she'll know how to style it so I can look my best." Sara continued to play with her hair, pulling one curl loose from the rest. "Mommy, please don't tell anyone. I don't wanna jinx my chances of getting it."

"I won't. My child, to me you are more than good enough. And they will accept you as you are," said Jen. "But you know your grandma wouldn't have agreed with those curls. She believed that a lady must look presentable—hair straight, clothes pressed, and legs crossed. Everything had to be in its place."

"I know, Mommy, but those were Granny's days, not mine."

"Yes, of course it was. But mind you, back then you wouldn't have been able to wear those curls and do the things you're doing. And believe me, Granny would have forced me under the hot comb. So count your blessings, my dear. Yes, you children and your new freedoms."

Jen picked the book up from the coffee table, turned it over in her hands, and traced the yellow aging stains on the corners. She opened the front cover and ran her fingers over her late husband's handwriting. *Property of Abram*, it read.

"Where did you find this?" Jen asked. "I thought your father threw this book out a long time ago. Jen thought back to the day Abram bought the book. She remembered how he haggled with one of the street booksellers in town and bragged afterward that he basically got the book for free. "Sometimes it felt like he loved this book more than he loved me." She laughed. "Did you know how much he loved this book?"

"Mm-hm," said Sara. "I remember how you would scold him for spending more time with the book than with you."

"I just know he would've been so proud of you. His own flesh and blood crossing the ocean to study." Looking at Sara, Jen saw the similarities in her smile to that of her late husband. A smile she hadn't seen on her daughter's face in a long time. "Your dad, he wanted to get out of this place, too. I always told him not to worry so much, because we could get out of here if we worked together, but he just never listened. Worked himself into his grave."

She shrugged. "'A man takes care of his family,'" he used to mumble when I tried to talk some sense into him."

"He gave me the book the night before he left us, Mommy."

Mother and daughter fell into a familiar silence, remembering the man they had lost. A man who took care of his family, one who left his house at the same time every morning and returned home at the same time every night, book in one hand, backpack in the other, and an expression on his face like he'd won the jackpot.

Jen sighed, put the book down on the coffee table, and moved closer to embrace her daughter. After a few seconds, she let go of Sara and used the armrest of the couch to get up. She touched the book and dried her eyes with a tissue. Sara understood the message of those tears. She knew they were not only in celebration of her but also of the memory of her father.

"What's burning, Mommy?" Sara teased because she knew that the kitchen was the one place that brought her mother endless joy. It was the only place that gave her back her light and life. After her father's passing, Sara had felt like she lost her mother as well as her father. Her friend Gershwin always reassured her when she complained that her mother no longer loved her. His words had helped her through her mother's mourning. He told her that her mother would get to the other side of her grief. He helped her to see that everyone mourns differently. Sara felt bad that she could never be to Gershwin what he was to her. She could never talk to him about the things he had to face with his mother, Rose, but Gershwin's life was complicated to say the least. Sometimes all you can do for someone else is just to be there when they need you.

"You've got time to make jokes?" said Jen as she rushed to the kitchen to finish cooking the samosas for her latest order. "Nothing's burning," Jen said loud enough for Sara to hear.

Sara's bubble of laughter was interrupted by Merle's chatter as she came through the front door. "Morning!" said Merle. "Where's the family this morning?" Merle Sanders had been their neighbour for the past twenty years. "Mmm, it smells great in here."

"Afternoon, Aunty Merle." Sara smiled at the middle-aged woman sticking her head into the living room. "I think the morning left us a long time ago." Sara's eyes darted to the clock hanging on the wall. "See for yourself, Aunty Merle."

"Always such a smarty-pants," Merle said. "When are you gonna tackle that bush on your head?" She laughed. "I mean, one of your best friends *is* a hairdresser. Why don't you ask Nique to do your hair?" she suggested, and walked off.

"I will, I will," Sara replied as she followed Merle to the kitchen. "But how are you, Mom Number Two?" she teased. "Why are you in such a hurry, or don't you have time for me today?"

"You're right, I have to deal with enough childish nonsense at home," Merle said. "That child of mine—I don't get why he doesn't get up and go find himself a job." Sara and Jen laughed at Merle's usual complaints about her youngest son who had dropped out of school.

"So Kyle's at home?" Sara asked. "Last night he bragged he was going to a house party in Main Road."

"Hmph, he's stretched out on the couch," Merle said. "I wish he would just go and find a job, but all he wants to do is lay on that couch the entire day, acting like I'm his personal chef. I don't know what's wrong with the children these days. Always this pain or that problem. You know what he did this morning? He walked into my room, telling me his back was aching and I needed to take these arthritic hands of mine and give him a massage." Merle removed her glasses to clean the oily smudges with the hem of her checkered apron. Sara and Jen watched Merle's every move, eagerly waiting for her to continue her story.

"Is this child crazy?" Merle asked no one in particular. "That husband of mine, he's been dead a long time. Kyle needs to go and find himself a wife. Things can't go on like this. Look at how comfortable Nique is living on her own, no need to ask anyone for anything."

Sara poured herself a glass of juice from the bottle in the fridge, pulled out the half a pint of milk for her mother and Merle, and sat down at the kitchen table.

Jen grabbed a plate full of uncooked samosas off the kitchen table and plopped them one after the other into hot oil. "The kettle just boiled before you walked in," Jen told Merle, as she lifted the golden-brown samosas out of the deep fryer and arranged them on a cooling rack.

29

Merle stood up from the kitchen table with a sigh and walked over to the cupboard standing next to the sink. She took out two mugs and tugged at the cupboard drawer. She eventually managed to open the drawer wide enough to remove a teaspoon, and then pushed the drawer back with too much strength so that the cupboard moved a few inches closer to the wall.

"Don't worry about that drawer, Merle," said Jen. "You know since Abram died everything in this house is broken."

"Girl, didn't you stop drinking coffee?" asked Merle, ignoring the pain she heard in her friend's voice. She added two heaped teaspoons of instant coffee to the mugs.

"I still take it in moderation," said Jen. "They say less is more." She put a plate of samosas on the table and cleaned her hands with a wet checkered dish towel. "I read somewhere that black coffee will remove the unwanted fat from around your thighs," said Jen as she smacked one of her love handles. She pulled out a chair and fell into it.

Merle took a sip of coffee and grabbed a samosa off the plate. "You can worry about losing weight. I don't," she said, and pinched two more samosas between her thumb and index finger from the shrinking mountain of pastries. "I'll drink my milky coffee and eat my samosas without any shame," she said, pushing another one into her mouth. She giggled when she noticed Sara watching her every move.

Merle wiped her fingers on the apron stretched around her body, pulled her coin purse from between her breasts, and took out two folded hundred-rand notes. "I didn't forget about you," she said, and pushed the money across the table. "Ley stopped by this morning and told me she wants to move back home. But how can I believe that? She stayed away for so long and suddenly she wants to come home like nothing happened. You would think there's trouble in paradise."

Sara smiled to herself and thought back to Merle's sixtieth birthday party when Merle stopped talking to her daughter, Ley, for an entire year after she found out that she was living with a woman. Sara sighed at the memory of her short relationship with Ley. It was quick and comfortable but ended painfully and their friendship was never the same again. Ley had wanted a serious relationship, but Sara was just experimenting because she'd always wondered what it would feel like to kiss a girl. *Imagine, me with another woman. What would people think about me? What would my mother think of me?*

"How do you expect me to accept your money," Jen said, and pushed the money back across the table to her friend. "How many times have you been here to help me with an order of samosas? There's a lot I couldn't have done without you. And besides, I still owe you for helping me with Pearl's order last week."

"Well, I'm not gonna argue. Just don't complain about me eating you bankrupt." Merle laughed. "And don't worry about paying me for helping you last week. Ley gave me enough cash to last for the rest of the month. She got a bonus, so she was generous handing out cash, even gave her brother a few notes. Besides, it's best if we can be there for one another. Life's too short." Merle finished her coffee and popped another samosa in her mouth.

"So when is Ley coming back?" Jen asked. "I wish she'd stopped by. I can't remember the last time I saw her. What does she say about her job?"

"No complaints," Merle said. "She's driving a new fancy car. It was part of her promotion. Can you believe it, Jen, my own daughter a detective?"

"Of course, I can. She always came home with one diploma or another," Jen said. "You must let her come home if she wants to. The city can be a lonely place. And visiting once a month isn't enough."

"Mm-hm, that's what I told her," said Merle. "But wait, have you heard about the body they found? Burned beyond recognition," she whispered.

"What, another body?" Jen asked.

"Sara, did you hear anything about it?" Merle asked. "They found the body on the rugby field, just like the others. That's why Ley was here this morning."

"Are you talking about the body they found last week in the bush?" asked Sara.

"No, they found another body this morning. Pitch-black and crispy. The people who found the body thought it was an animal, until they saw the skull," said Merle. "According to Ley, that friend of yours is missing."

"Aunty Merle, who are you talking about?"

"The gay one that's on meth."

"Are you talking about Carl?" asked Sara.

"Yes, that's his name," Merle said, and pushed her grey hair back under her paisley headscarf. "Ley told me to ask you if you've seen him because his sister is calling her non-stop looking for him."

"But Aunty Merle, Carl isn't gay. People should stop making up stories, and you should stop believing those stories."

"But if everyone tells the same story, then you must listen," Merle said.

Sara rolled her eyes. "But I just saw him on Sunday," she said. "Pushing a shopping cart down Main Road with Toothless walking next to him. They were probably collecting scraps to sell at the scrapyard."

"I don't know anything about that, but Ley said she visited Nique before she came by to see me, and Nique hasn't seen Carl in the last week. I told Ley to come see you herself, but her day was too full. She's always too busy." Merle sighed as she used the table to hoist herself out of the kitchen chair. "Ooh, I need a new pair of knees," she said, and walked over to the freshly fried samosas sitting on the cooling rack. "Ley wanted to know if I gave Carl's sister her number. Said she doesn't know where that woman got her number from." She put the cooled samosas in a container lined with wax paper. "Apparently, she keeps on calling, and Ley said half the time she can't understand what the woman's saying through her drunk mumbling." Merle put the last samosa from the cooling rack into her mouth.

"Aunty Merle, are you sure Ley said Carl is missing?"

Sara asked. "Are you really sure that's what she said?" Merle was everyone's aunt. She was the aunt everyone on their street could hear praying every morning, but she was also the aunt everyone knew added details to the stories she heard. The aunt who always had to taste one last samosa before she walked home.

"That's what she said. If you don't believe me, you can call her and ask her yourself," said Merle.

Sara scoffed and left the two older women in the kitchen laughing and chatting about the pastor's wife, Pearl, who still needed to pay for the extra batch of samosas Jen had added to her order. She took her cellphone from her pocket and checked her data balance as she walked into her bedroom. Her phone vibrated with a carrier message. "Ninety cents," Sara read the message out loud. "What can I do with ninety cents?" She pulled a ten-rand note out from under a bunch of coins lying on her desk and walked to the corner shop next door to top up her airtime.

She knew all her hard work would eventually take her out of the Shadows. It wasn't that she didn't like living here. All her friends were here, a boy she'd met recently, her family. And it wasn't like there weren't any real opportunities in Cape Town. But most of the time it felt like the poverty and oppression that ran through the streets of the Shadows couldn't care less about her big dreams.

3

AT THE SHEBEEN

Monday

Nique waved as her cousin pulled away from her front gate. She never could've imagined that Ley would visit her to look for Carl. Nique hadn't thought much of it when Carl didn't come to see her. She'd asked him many times to bring his laundry over; he always said yes but never did. So him not visiting wasn't anything new to her. She always knew that he would spin some story about why he couldn't make it. Nique turned and walked back inside, closed the front door, locked it, and went into her bedroom to fetch a fresh pack of cigarettes. Back in the living room, she threw herself onto one of the couches, lit a cigarette, and relaxed, as she had no hair appointments to get ready for that day.

The last time she saw Carl was a week ago at Byron's Shebeen. That Sunday, she had made double sure that she locked her door. She had walked out her gate expecting to see her neighbours, the two sisters who lived next door, but they weren't in their usual spot. It was their Sunday ritual to sit in their yard on upside-down beer crates on either side of a small table where a two-litre bottle filled with water would stand. But that was just a front. Scared that the local pastor would walk by and judge them for drinking, they used the water bottle to conceal an open beer bottle and two small glasses filled with beer that they would hide when someone passed in the street. They normally stayed out there from early in the day until long after sunset. Nique always enjoyed their playful banter. She had looked at their house for any sign of life, but all the windows and doors had been closed. She had hoped everything was okay, as they were in their late sixties. Nique later found out that there had been a birth in their family.

As usual, Nique had gone to Byron's Shebeen for their regular Sunday visit where they would watch movies, talk, and fuck for most of the evening. It was their weekly lovers' ritual. Nique knew what it took to run a business like Byron's, but she couldn't help asking him every other week to visit her and leave Clint, his second-in-command, in charge for a few hours. Byron would just shrug and tell her that it wasn't Clint's business or responsibility. He always reminded her that he had a business to run, and that none of his soldiers had the brains to do what was needed. She knew he didn't trust anyone, not even the woman he had married and had two sons with.

She never spoke to her friends about her relationship with the biggest thug in the Shadows, but every corner in the Shadows had eyes. That day, she had taken her normal route to Byron's Shebeen and, as usual, everyone she walked past said hello. Her door-to-door hairdresser business brought her clients from every street in the Shadows, and she was well known and well respected. She had smiled, but she felt the same shame and guilt every week. Everyone knew that the two of them were dating. Even his wife knew.

Nique went to the kitchen, switched the kettle on, and listened to the laughter coming from the kitchen next door. Byron always told Nique that she shouldn't worry about his business with his wife, that they had an understanding, but she could never make peace with the fact that she was dating a married man with two kids. When she was in high school, she had always wondered where Byron got the money to fix up his mother's house while he was in jail. Many people took part in spreading the gossip that meth addicts killed his mother, but no one knew the real story of what happened to her. Byron got out of prison six months after his mother's death and moved into her house with two of his soldiers and four dogs. That's all he'd had, or that's what it had looked like to Nique. She later found out that he had sent his wife and two kids to go and live with her mother.

The water in the kettle boiled. Nique filled a blue hot

water flask, trying to save on her electric bill, and poured the rest into a mug with her usual two spoons of coffee and no sugar. She pulled a box of rusks from the cupboard and put two side by side on a plate. She picked up the mug with one hand and the plate with the other and walked back to the living room.

Nique remembered the first time she had hooked up with Byron. It was her second-to-last year in high school. Gershwin, Carl, and Sara had decided to go to class, but Nique had felt like a day off and joined a group of her school friends who were ditching. They had decided they needed beer to make the afternoon more exciting. Nique was tasked with going to Byron's house to buy beer because she looked the oldest. She collected the money from those who could contribute, and they only had enough money for four beers. They didn't have money to pay the extra fee shebeens charged for buying beer without a beer bottle, so Nique left her group of school friends standing on the corner and hoisted the backpack with the empty bottles over her shoulder, clasping it under her arm to stop the glass from clinking. She felt brave because everyone else was too scared to go to the don's place. She walked fearlessly past the barking dogs next to Byron's front door, knocked, and waited anxiously. When one of Byron's soldiers, with gang tattoos on his face, answered the door, she just stared and couldn't speak. The guy asked what she wanted, and she took a few seconds before she informed him that she wanted to buy beer.

She was invited inside, and the house smelled distinctly of dirty ashtrays mixed with beer. Byron, slumped over on the couch in the living room, was busy rolling a blunt. He asked her why she wasn't in school. She lied and told him they were writing exams and it was their day off. He laughed coarsely when she confidently said she was old enough to drink. He told her that day if she stayed to enjoy a drink with him, he would give her anything she wanted. She was unsure but stayed because her school friends were depending on her to bring the beer for their day off.

Byron told his two guards to go feed the dogs. One of them tried to say they had already fed them, but one stare from Byron cut his sentence in half. Nique hurried through her first beer, emptying the glass before Byron could put the beer bottle down. Her head started spinning. She told him that her friends were waiting on her. He said nothing and took her hand in his. He told her she was beautiful. He touched her flushed cheeks, and she told him again that she needed to leave because her friends were waiting. She didn't like where things were going, but she was also intrigued to see the big don so vulnerable in front of her. She was scared that Byron would hit her if he found out that she had a dick between her legs. The fact that she found him attractive made her uncomfortable. He asked if he could kiss her. She told him once again that she needed to go, but he didn't listen. His grip tightened on her hand, and he pulled it to his mouth and started kissing it. She said no, but Byron took what he wanted. She tried lying and telling him that she had a boyfriend, but slowly she stopped fighting him because there was something intriguing about the man she saw.

Nique touched her cheeks as they flared up at the memory. She remembered that day like it was yesterday because it had happened in her previous life, before her operation. She was still putting pantyhose stuffed with tissues in her bra and standing to pee when she had to use a public toilet. She remembered the shivers she felt running through Byron when he felt what she had between her legs. She remembered him hardening through his pants as he pushed up against her. She remembered how scared she was when she saw the pleasure dancing in Byron's eyes when he forced himself on her. Sometimes she still saw that sliver of excitement in his eyes. His eyes always told her the stories his lips never could. He never spoke about the evils he had to do to keep what he had, but she could always see the pain struggling in his eyes. What scared her more was the intense longing she felt to feel him inside of her. She was shocked when he told her she didn't have to be shy or scared because she was exactly what he was looking for.

That day was the first and last time Nique tried to push Byron away. She struggled to get away, but the more she struggled, the harder he fought her. Then she looked him straight in the eyes and stopped struggling. He stopped. He pushed himself off her, got up from the couch they were sitting on, took the glass standing on the table, poured himself another beer, and told her she must leave. He called one of his men and told him to add four more beers to her load no charge. And that's where it started for the two of them. He helped her get what she wanted, and she gave him what he craved. He helped her with her first payment for her top surgery. She was there when his wife and kids weren't, which was most of the time. She made it clear she needed their relationship to be kept quiet, and she didn't want any special treatment. He needed to treat her the same way he treated everyone else in the Shadows. That was why she still waited for the bouncers to tell her if she could enter Byron's shebeen when she visited.

Nique's phone screen lit up. It was Gershwin. He told her in a WhatsApp message that his mother was in one of her moods, so he wouldn't stop by and he'd see her on Thursday. Nique didn't reply to Gershwin's message. Her thoughts travelled back to the previous week when she had seen his mother at the shebeen. The bar was full that night. From outside in the street, she could hear the clinking of beer bottles through the blasting music. Two heavy-set bouncers stood in their usual spots, one on each side of the black entrance. The light above the signage flickered on, illuminating the locally made sign telling everyone who passed that it was BYRON'S SHEBEEN. The front yard was full of people sitting on empty beer cases and leaning against the inside of the black-painted fence, waiting their turn to enter. Some stood in small groups, passing a beer or a lit cigarette or joint. People were pushing through the entrance of the yard like sheep to be slaughtered.

Every man who wanted to enter the premises had to endure a rough body search because the only people allowed to have weapons or drugs were Byron, his soldiers, and Clint. A quarrel erupted that night when a guy refused to be searched because the women walked in without going through the same humiliation. Then there was the guy she came close to smacking for touching her ass. She still felt dirty any time she thought of it. Byron had gotten angry and scolded her for not informing his bouncers of the pervert. Nique smiled as she remembered Byron insisting that no one could touch her but him.

She hadn't thought anything of the angry voice she'd heard when she arrived, thinking it was just a normal Sunday evening at Byron's Shebeen. She couldn't see what was going on or where it came from, as the light coming from inside the gambling room painted everyone standing in front as silhouettes. But before she knew it, Gershwin's mother, Rose, had pushed Nique out of the way, screaming at the top of her lungs that every dog has their day, but pigs like them would be slaughtered and burned at the altar. Rose scolded the man filling the frame of the gambling room's door and reminded them all they would burn in hell. Nique was shocked. What was the biggest Christian in the Shadows doing exiting the gambling room at the shebeen? Nique immediately tried to hide from being spotted by the devil herself and dodged behind a group of men rambling on about rugby. Nique fought with herself. On the one hand, she didn't want Gershwin to get any more shit because of Rose's hatred of Nique. But on the other hand, Rose was the one who should be ashamed of herself for being there. Nique decided that taking a picture of Rose would suit her better than hiding from her. She needed evidence because neither Gershwin nor Sara would ever believe her without it. Nique called out to Rose, who turned around just as the power at the shebeen cut out. When the solar-powered floodlights switched on Nique stood close enough to Rose to take a picture.

Nique navigated to her cellphone's gallery and clicked on the photo. She laughed at Rose's scrunched-up face looking straight into the camera lens. Nique laughed at the angry frown she recognized on Rose's forehead, one she'd had to endure on every visit she made to Gershwin's house. How could Rose be so stupid as to let herself get caught at a shebeen by the one person she hated most, maybe even more than she hated her own son? Nique was sure that Rose would tell everybody that she was there to give the sinners a chance to repent and turn their hearts over to Jesus. Nique felt guilty for not telling Gershwin. She knew she had to, but how was she supposed to do it? She felt guilty and ashamed for her weekly Sunday visits with a married man. She couldn't forget about Byron's wife and kids who always had to fight to spend time with him. Nique tried talking some sense into him, telling him he should spend more time with his family, but he made it clear to her that nothing was more important to him than his business. Byron never worried about his wife knowing about his flings with other women, but Nique never wanted her to know about Byron's relationship with her. But she also knew that you couldn't hide anything in the Shadows. Someone always found out.

That Sunday evening Nique had done what she did every week. She had bought a couple of ciders and found her corner table in the back of the shebeen empty, like they always kept it for her on Sundays. The back of the shebeen had been unusually quiet that night, like everyone was congregating in the front yard. She had been pouring herself a glass of cider when Clint walked in, Carl following like a scared dog cowering behind its master, head bowed and tail tucked between its legs. Clint had walked straight to her table and Nique had only been able to see Carl's face when he stepped out of Clint's big shadow. She had found it strange that Carl didn't look at her or greet her. She had tried to meet his eyes, but they were searching the cracks in the cement floor for things that weren't there. She had gotten angry and scolded Clint for always using Carl for jobs and never treating him right. It wasn't the first time; she had even tried talking to Byron about it, but he'd explained that no one was using Carl. He was working for them.

Clint had left to attend to something behind the bar and Carl had stood in front of her for a while, almost like he was trying to figure out what to do next. Finally, he had taken a seat across from Nique at her table and she'd asked him if he wanted a smoke. He'd nodded while scratching in his pants pockets. She had pushed her pack of cigarettes over to him, but he'd continued searching his pockets. Nique had tried to get him to talk. She'd asked him if something was the matter. He'd looked at Clint, who was leaning against the wall on the other side of the shebeen, and lit a cigarette. Then Clint had come to fetch her, telling her that Byron was ready to see her. She had left Carl there with a few cigarettes, and that was the last time she saw him. Carl hadn't said anything when she'd left, but he'd given her a look that made her feel uneasy for the rest of the night. Maybe if she had stayed with him a little longer, she would know where he was right now.

4

THE DEACON

Monday

Rose Lawrence picked up the mug of coffee Gershwin had made for her. She took a big gulp but spat most of it back into the mug. "Are you trying to poison me?" she shouted at the closed bedroom door of her only child. "You call this coffee? Can't even make a proper cup of coffee!"

Her attention locked on to the top half of the kitchen door being pushed open and closed by the early winter breeze. Annoyed, she banged the door closed. The force of the door slamming into its frame shook the rest of the doors in the house. She pulled out a kitchen chair and threw herself into it. She made every movement with the express purpose of showing her son that she was not planning on settling down anytime soon.

"When your grandmother was still alive you had manners. What did I do wrong to bring a child like you into this world?" scolded Rose. "When you want something, you get it. And now look at me. Having to beg you for everything." Rose grabbed her coffee. Forgetting that just moments before she had spat half of what she'd drunk back into the mug, she took another swig, immediately followed by more spitting.

She got up and threw her half-full cup of coffee in the already full sink. The oily brown water grew darker as the coffee mixed with the dirty water swimming around yesterday's dishes. She wiped the spit she felt drying under her chin and hobbled on her bad foot over to Gershwin's closed bedroom door. "So you think you're old enough to not follow my rules? I think it's time you got the fuck out of my house!" shouted Rose, banging ferociously on the door. "I hope you're fucking listening. I want you out. Useless piece of shit!" She moved away from Gershwin's bedroom, defeated by the silence coming from the other side of the door. It was a tired but daily ritual she enacted with her son, the victim.

The shuffle to her room was a short one. Music screamed out of Gershwin's bedroom in time with Rose's dragging steps. Rose's anger at what her own mother had done found new footing in her mind every time she attacked her son. *I never wanted it to be like this*, she thought. She never wanted to be this way with him, but he pushed her away every chance he got, and all she tried to do was show him how to live his life. She tried to help him to not end up the way his friends had ended up. Like that devil himself who had messed with God's handiwork and turned himself into a woman. *How dare he?* she thought.

Rose had stopped taking down the portrait of her mother and father that always hung in the same spot in the hallway for as long as she could remember. She had tried hiding it, but Gershwin made it his job to find it and hang it back in its place. Every time she took it down and hid it, the next day it would find its way back. It was like her parents' ghosts were haunting every corner of her house. She knew Gershwin would never understand what she went through every time she saw her parents smiling back at her. She even tried burning the framed photograph of her parents, but it was like their ghosts lived in Gershwin, and he plucked the photograph from the flames. No one would understand how Gershwin's eyes, his smile, brought her father back to life, and no one cared. *It's just Pastor Richard, who cares about me*, she thought.

Rose resented Gershwin because her own mother had pushed her away. She couldn't help that her father had used his daughter as his second wife. It didn't matter what she did; her father came back every night, and her mother never stopped him. Rose tried hiding her body with oversized clothing, but nothing helped. It didn't matter how much weight she put on. Even after she almost lost her foot when a minibus taxi ran her over, her father still came back to her bed. She couldn't push him away, no matter how hard she tried. And where was her mother? Cowering inside her Bible. And then Rose's mother had turned around to raise Gershwin as if he was her son and not the shame brought on by Rose's father sexually abusing her. Her mother could never be the Christian she was, Rose thought. *God wants his disciples to do his work, even if it means getting demon blood on your hands.*

Rose unlocked her bedroom door with a key she pulled from her apron pocket. The door's hinges squeaked as it swung open. She was used to the mouldy air that welcomed her every time she walked into her bedroom. Rose shuffled slowly past the stacked cardboard boxes, filled with old shoes and hand-me-downs, to get to her bed. She kept telling Gershwin to stay out of her bedroom, but he never listened to her, and even though she locked her door, he always found a way in. She knew he stole from her. Her medication and money disappeared when she wasn't home. She knew he stole the food she hid in her bedroom cupboard.

When Gershwin had turned eighteen, she decided to cut him off because he needed to make his own way. She didn't understand why he wouldn't give her extra money to help with the electricity and water bills. She also needed to win back the money she'd lost at Byron's Shebeen. She was convinced their machines were rigged. She'd never doubled her money, and the only people she ever saw win big were the ones who worked for Byron. Byron won the biggest, but she'd show him. Her time would come.

Rose sat on her bed and counted the big church hats on top of her cupboard. She knew if she spun a good enough story for the sisters at her church, she could sell them a few of the hats. *Every good Christian woman needs her hats*, she thought. Rose didn't go to church to be pretentious in front of the congregation. She dressed up for Jesus and Pastor Richard. Rose smiled dreamily at the fantasy of her and Pastor Richard lying in bed kissing. She knew that Jesus and Pastor Richard would reward her for the things she was doing, but Gershwin made her life a living hell. If he weren't here, her life would be better. If Gershwin didn't change his devilish ways, she'd need to speak to Pastor Richard about sacrificing him. She wouldn't mind adding him to the Cleansing. She was a little worried about the burnt-out body that was found on the rugby field this morning, but it couldn't be the one from last night. *We buried that body*, she thought.

She swung her heavy legs onto the unmade double bed. Her head sank into the soft pillow and she smelled the men's deodorant she sprayed on the case. *Pastor Richard loves me. He said so himself*, she thought as she closed her eyes. "I have nothing to worry about," she whispered to herself. "Jesus protects us against the evils out there."

Rose fell into a doze but was quickly pulled out of it when she heard Gershwin's music quiet down and his bedroom door open.

"What are you doing in my kitchen?" she screamed. She pushed herself up on her elbows and listened to Gershwin's footsteps scurry into the bathroom.

The bathroom door closed. The hissing silence grew louder in her ears as she listened for any further sounds coming from the other side of her closed bedroom door. Getting up now was too much trouble. After a few minutes of hearing nothing, she relaxed back onto her bed. She closed her eyes and thought again about Pastor Richard. If his wife were out of the way, she could give him everything he deserved. Rose could give him a better life. Maybe if Rose got rid of the child she had been forced to have, Pastor Richard would see that she was worthy and leave his wife for her.

Rose disappeared deeper into her thoughts and wandered off into a morning nap.

BLARING MUSIC OUTSIDE HER bedroom window dragged Rose from her slumber. She jumped up as fast as her body would allow to give the culprit a piece of her mind, but as she opened her window, the minibus taxi moved off with the door operator whistling at a couple walking on the other side of the street and shouting, "Town? Need a ride?"

"Fucking people! Why are they making noise so early in the morning?" complained Rose. "Don't they know some of us need our sleep?"

She shut the window and fell back onto her bed. She fluffed her pillow, getting ready to continue her nap, missing the arrival of a red car at her front gate. A man got out, swinging a brown leather messenger's bag over his right shoulder. He greeted Rose's neighbours with a big smile as he pressed the button on his key fob. The car's alarm and door locks beeped and clicked simultaneously.

"Morning, Pastor," said a woman walking by.

Pastor Richard greeted the member of his congregation and pushed open Rose's gate like he lived there. He knew Rose never used her front door, which was permanently blocked by a big rotting TV cabinet, and walked down the side of the house. As he passed the open living room window, he recognized the mouldy stink he always smelled when Rose stood too close to him at a church service. The smell of Rose's house was one of the reasons why his wife wouldn't set foot inside it. The other reason was Gershwin. The prayer meetings at Rose's house were always the shortest.

When Pastor Richard reached the kitchen door he knocked softly. After his first knock went unanswered, he cleared his throat, pasted a smile on his face, and knocked again. He listened attentively, his ears searching for the sounds of Rose's shuffling gait.

"Morning, Deacon Rose!" Pastor Richard sang out, trying to sound sincere. He knocked again, but after there was still no answer, he walked back to the front of the house.

"Morning, Deacon Rose?" Pastor Richard called again, hoping Rose wasn't home so that he could get on with the real reason he was visiting. When he returned to the kitchen door once again, his desire for Gershwin to be the only one there was dampened when he heard Rose's shuffling walk.

Inside the house, unaware of her guest knocking at the kitchen door, Rose pulled on her almost new pink-checkered apron, which was a few sizes too small for her. The material stretched tightly over her shoulders as she shuffled past the cardboard boxes stacked against the wall next to her bed. She tied the checkered apron around her waist as she left her bedroom and finally heard the knocking at her kitchen door.

"Yes! Who's there?" she shouted.

The knocking came a little louder than before.

"Who's there?" she screamed again. When she finally reached the kitchen door, she fought with the key in the lock, rattling it. Finally, she pulled the door open, only to realize that the door had been unlocked the entire time. She then remembered not locking it before she went to sleep.

Rose gasped when she saw the pastor standing in front of her. She was surprised to see him visiting her because he never came to her house alone. "Pastor?! Good morning! Come inside. If I knew it was you standing at the door, I would've opened it sooner." Rose giggled uncomfortably. She touched her cheeks flaming with desire and embarrassment. *I hope he didn't hear me cuss*, she thought, thinking back to the taxi with loud music that woke her from her nap. "You know children these days don't have any respect. They've been knocking at my door at ungodly hours, and then when I answer, no one's there. If their parents taught them to behave better, they wouldn't be pranking older people." Her eyes travelled over the man dressed in blue jeans, a white T-shirt, black Nikes, and a black leather jacket as he walked through her kitchen door.

"I thought you weren't at home," said Pastor Richard. "Been knocking at the door for a while now. Even checked the front door, even though I know you don't use it anymore."

"Oh, I'm so sorry for keeping you waiting, Pastor," said Rose. "I feel so bad. Come sit. Let me get you something to drink." She pulled out one of the kitchen chairs. "I was busy cleaning in my room," lied Rose.

"I'm sorry for popping in unannounced, but I tried calling. I tried your cellphone first, and when you didn't answer, I called Gershwin's cellphone, but he didn't answer either," said Pastor Richard, ignoring the darkness that moved over Rose's face when she heard her son's name. "I thought you didn't want to talk to me today, so I had to stop by." He grinned. "Choir business." Pastor Richard placed his messenger bag on the kitchen table and opened the flap. Rose sat down across from him, her eyes dodging anxiously between his hand digging through the bag and his face.

"Jesus is blessing us with good weather today," said Pastor Richard. He never liked the way Rose looked at him. He tried to settle into the chair, but it was hard for him to feel comfortable around her. That's why he never visited her on his own, and if he needed something from her he would call her. But today he had to let Gershwin know that he needed to see him. He couldn't stop the shiver of disgust he felt whenever Rose touched him. She always went out of her way to touch him. He didn't even allow his wife, Pearl, to touch him the way Rose imposed herself on his body. He had no need to worry about Pearl wanting any intimacy from him anymore because all she was looking for after their child's death was money she could spend freely. Money was her comfort. The loss of their only child was too much for their marriage. They blamed each other for the drowning and everything fell apart, starting with their intimacy. The money and status that came with his position in the church were the only reasons Pearl stayed with him. Church business was good business. But he also felt grateful for Rose's desire for him. This way he could manipulate her however he wanted. He enjoyed it when people went out of their way to please him. It turned him on when his flock danced around to his every word.

"Can I get you some coffee?" Rose asked, interrupting Pastor Richard's search through his bag. She walked over to the old kitchen cupboard standing against the wall. "The water is still hot. Pastor, you like your coffee black with two sugars, right?" Rose started her task without waiting for the pastor to answer. "I'm so glad you stopped by. I wanted to speak to you about Gershwin. I don't know what to do with him anymore," she said, forgetting about making coffee and sitting down again. "He won't help me around the house, and he acts like he's doing me a favour giving me a bit of money," she complained.

Eyes and hands frantically scouring through his leather bag, Pastor Richard pulled out a large white envelope and set it to one side.

"It looks like you need a bigger bag, Pastor." Rose smiled as Pastor Richard unzipped the front of the bag to check the smaller pockets.

"I'm sure I packed it," he said as he removed a beige cellphone. He wished Pearl would stop complaining about her missing phone.

"Did Brother Calvin say anything about the Cleansing?" asked Rose, recognizing the cellphone she had used a few nights before. She picked it up and smiled at the memory of their deeds.

"Brother Calvin was supposed to remove the video from the cellphone today, but he called me earlier to tell me he has the flu." Pastor Richard sighed with relief as his fingers felt the outline of the thumb drive. "It seems it got stuck between the fabric lining and the leather." He laughed, and repacked the beige cellphone in the bag. He put the white envelope in front of him and placed the thumb drive on top of it.

"Did he say anything else about what happened after we finished?"

"It's what he didn't say, Deacon Rose," said Pastor Richard. "But maybe I'm making too big a thing about nothing."

"So the body they found this morning…"

"We have nothing to worry about, Deacon Rose," said Pastor Richard. "Brother Calvin assured me that it wasn't the offering. He said that a story was going around that it was one of the gangsters in South Street that was killed using the necklace method."

"That's when they put a tire around the neck and light it on fire?"

"Yes, that's the story," he said. "They necklaced him. If only they knew that we were doing God's work."

"God is good." Rose sighed and stood up again to make the coffee. "He knows what He's doing. Cleaning the Shadows of all the evil in our community. I knew there was nothing for me to worry about. All I needed to do was trust and believe. Byron is the next offering. Don't you think that will make Jesus happy with us?"

Rose scooped heaped teaspoons of coffee and sugar into two cups. Pastor Richard counted as she dumped one spoon of sugar after the other into the first mug. One, two, three, four. Pastor Richard's brow crinkled with worry as he thought about the heaped teaspoons on their way to his arteries. He remembered what his doctor had said: "Less sugar, Pastor."

"Two teaspoons are enough, Deacon Rose," said Pastor Richard, his hand stretched out to keep Rose from dumping more sugar into the second mug.

Rose shuffled over to the white electric kettle, ensuring that she rubbed Pastor Richard's back as she moved past him. *He feels and smells so nice*, she thought.

"I still have some cake left. The church sister down the street brought it over last night," said Rose, as she placed a steaming cup of coffee in front of Pastor Richard.

"I can't stay long," he said apologetically, and shifted closer to the table. Pastor Richard smiled to hide his uneasiness. "There's still a lot that needs to happen before the next Cleansing ceremony, and I want to get all the planning done."

"You still need to eat," said Rose. "It doesn't look like you get enough to eat at home. Just give me a minute. I'll fetch it quickly." She scrambled out of the kitchen, ignoring the pastor's hands silently protesting.

Pastor Richard sighed in defeat and tasted his coffee. He spat it right back into the mug, jumped out of his chair, and rushed over to throw the coffee into the half-filled kitchen sink. He watched as the dirty water turned darker.

Rose returned and placed a Styrofoam food container on the kitchen table. She bent down in front of the kitchen cupboard and pulled out a saucer.

"Oh, is your coffee done already, Pastor?" she asked.

"Yes, thank you, Deacon Rose. It was tasty, just how I like it." His eyes flicked nervously between the murky water in the kitchen sink and the empty mug standing in front of him. "Deacon Rose, will you lead the meeting tonight? Brother Calvin was supposed to do it, but it doesn't look like he'll be able to, what with the flu and all. Everything we spoke about in our last meeting is in the envelope," Richard said, pointing with his eyes at the white envelope on the table in front of him. "I also wrote a few things down I'd like you to talk about."

"But, Pastor, won't you be there?" asked Rose, her brows pulled together with concern. She wiped her cake-crumbed fingers on the front of her checkered apron.

"You'll be fine, Deacon Rose. Don't look so worried. I have so much to do today. I would really appreciate it if you could do this for me. Deacon Calvin won't be able to get the video off the cellphone, and we can't ask Gershwin, so I'll have to figure out a way to do it myself," Richard said, his thoughts jumping to his wife's cellphone stashed in his bag. "And then there's choir practice tomorrow after the prayer meeting. Gershwin can help with that. Please give him the thumb drive. He needs to bring it to my house tomorrow. "I sent him a WhatsApp message. He hasn't responded, but I'm sure he'll check his WhatsApp later and know what time and what to do with it," said Richard, looking forward to his wife's departure the next day to visit her sister for the rest of the week. He smiled knowing that he wouldn't have to worry about cutting his time short with Gershwin.

"I'll make sure he gets it. And don't worry, I'll make sure he brings it to you tomorrow," said Rose. She threw the last bit of her coffee in the kitchen sink. Pastor Richard watched the dirty water rise. Rose touched the back of her headscarf. *I need to wash my hair before tonight's meeting*, she thought. She hoped the pastor couldn't smell the beer and cigarette smoke on her. That's what disgusted her most about the shebeen, the fumes that followed you when you left, like a curse dogging your every step, pulling you back.

"The Cleansing last night was our best so far, don't you think, Pastor?" Rose said. A smile crept across her aging face.

"Yes, that's right," Pastor Richard said. "But we can't wait so long before we do the next one. A week was too long. What if someone had found him there? I heard his sister was looking for him everywhere. She even went to the cops. Next time, everything must be in place for us to do it immediately. That way we don't have to worry about what happens to the body after we're done with the offering," he whispered. "If they had only dug the grave when I asked them to do it, then everything would've been sorted out."

"But Pastor, where did they end up burying the body?" asked Rose.

"If I tell you, you'll have to be our next offering." Pastor Richard laughed. "I'm just joking, Deacon Rose. God wants us to only offer up sinners. They said they buried the body deeper in the bush where no one will find it."

"That's good, Pastor. God will bless all of us and the Shadows for the offerings we're giving Him," said Rose, a nervous smile spreading across her face. "Yes, that's right, we did what was right for Him," she said.

Pastor Richard cleared his throat and pushed his chair back, picked up his messenger bag off the table, and rested it on his lap. "Thank you for the coffee, Deacon Rose, but I must get going," he said, standing up.

"But Pastor, what about the cake?" Rose asked as a last attempt to keep the man of her dreams with her for a little bit longer.

"I'll take a rain check, Deacon Rose," said Richard. "Next time we'll make more time for some cake and another cup of your delicious coffee," he lied, and walked toward the kitchen door.

Rose shuffled after him like a lapdog. "I'll give it to him now," she said, looking down at the blue thumb drive she was holding. Her eyes turned sad and dark when Pastor Richard walked out without another word. She closed the kitchen door. At the same time Gershwin's bedroom door flung open, like he was waiting for the guest to leave. He ignored his mother's bad-tempered face and focused on the thumb drive she threw on the kitchen table.

"He said you'd know what to do with it," Rose said. "And you better make sure you take it to him early tomorrow morning. Not everyone can have your life of sleeping the entire day away and doing nothing."

Gershwin smiled as he picked up the thumb drive, pushed it into his jeans back pocket, and walked off to the bathroom. He shut out his mother's scolding, touched his pocket, and smiled again.

5

THE DRAGON

Last Tuesday

My headstone will read, *Here lies Carl Bosman, the one who was led to his death.* They never teach you the right things at school, like how to free yourself from being tied up. I've tried everything, but the more I struggled to free my arms from the wires, the tighter they cut into my skin. So I gave up. Now I'm just sitting here, quietly waiting for someone to come and save me. Maybe if I stay quiet they'll forget I'm here.

My sister's probably harassing everyone, trying to find me. Not for anything other than money. The money she believes I owe her for living with her in my mother's house. She's probably going crazy breaking anything of mine she can find. Not that I have much, but I kept small worthless trinkets that reminded me of Mom. But money is the only thing Mandy cares about. When my sister started going on about money this and money that, I got up and left. Even though I had just gotten back from help-ing Clint. All my sister ever wanted was money. All she ever talked and argued about was money, always acting like it was her house, but Mom left it to both of us. I get it. Alcohol is just like meth; it's just that one's legal and the other isn't. But Mandy has no one to blame but herself that they took her two kids away. She can blame Aunty Nita for calling CPS, but it's Mandy's own fault that it got to that point. And when I say no to giving her money, her bulldog of a boyfriend has the nerve to start barking off promises of never-ending beatings. Every time they start acting up I tell myself, *Carl, just shut up and go.* So that's what I did.

I left Mandy to go and see if Clint would pay me for the work I'd done for him the night before. I shouldn't have waited to ask him because then I wouldn't have met Toothless standing on the corner with his shitty ideas. When I found Clint at Byron's Shebeen there was some-thing off about him. Instead of speaking to me, he just pointed at things that he wanted me to carry in or remove from the van. And when that job was done, I reminded him that he still owed me for the last one. He scolded me, asking if I thought he was a thief, and couldn't I see he had company? Referring to the women hanging on him. When women congregate around Clint, it's like he sees nothing other than the pussy around him. There's nothing

I can do to get him to pay me what's mine. I mean, you can't go around telling your boss when you want your pay. That's not how this world works. But Clint, he's not like the rest. He'll help me out if I ask, most of the time. But, you know, pussy's status is higher than mine.

Before I could answer Clint's question, he told me to leave. So I left. I thought if I asked Nique for some money to shut my sister up she would help me, but she wasn't home. The front door and all the windows were closed. That's when I saw Toothless standing on the corner of Nique's street, his eyes scurrying all over like he was looking for his next victim.

I wish I had taken another route. Then Toothless wouldn't have seen me and gotten me to go along with him. Then I wouldn't be here now, tied to a fucking tree with a musty-smelling tarp over my head. Regret always shows up when the shit's stinking right up in your face.

Come to think of it, it's my sister's and Toothless's fault that I'm sitting here. Money! It's always about money with them.

I spotted Toothless from a mile away, with the shiny bald patch in the middle of his head, almost like he put too much hair gel on his hair. He could've gone far with sports, but I guess that wasn't part of the life plan God had for him. Toothless was quarrelling with Pete, who lived next door to Gershwin. I don't understand why Toothless keeps hanging out with him. Toothless never stops complaining about Pete, but when you look for Toothless, you'll always find him next to Pete, busy smoking Mandrax in a white pipe or sharing a meth pipe.

When I was still a few feet away from them, Toothless flipped out and gave Pete a backhand. I could hear the hand landing on his cheek down the street. I almost walked past them, but Toothless turned around and saw me. He fell in step and continued walking with me. There was no getting rid of Toothless. He said nothing. Didn't greet me or nothing. I asked Toothless why he smacked Pete, but he just ignored me, and we continued walking in silence for a bit. Then he asked me if I had something on me to fix his low. I lied and told him I'd used up everything, but I had half a straw in my pocket. You must always look out for yourself. He sighed and told me I was just as useless as Pete, who didn't want to go with him and look for scraps at the train yard.

We kept walking in silence, until I decided to tell him that I still needed to get my money from Clint. Toothless said, "Fuck Clint! Come with me. I know where we can score." He said we wouldn't have any trouble getting in and out. He promised he'd give me half, but I knew he would go back on his word like he did a few weeks back. But I had nothing to lose. A score is a score, even if it's just a small cut, but half sounded even better. And look at me now.

Toothless believed that meth was the only thing that would silence his endless hunger, but his granny taught him that he had to work if he wanted to eat. Even if that work meant stealing from his granny, then that's what he would do. But I agree with Toothless's granny—if you want to eat, then you have to work for it. Mom always gave me everything I needed. I was her "baby boy." My sister hated me for it. It took me a while to think like Toothless. After Mom was gone, I was still waiting to be fed, so I did things I'm not proud of. Sometimes we do stupid things to get what we think is ours.

I had told Toothless we should sell wood. That's an honest living. That way we wouldn't have to steal scrap metal from the train yards. He said he couldn't care less. I told him we would be filling a gap in the market because the people living in the Shadows would buy the wood. I tried explaining that people would buy anything they could get for cheap. But Toothless never listened to me. He told me that people would never buy from druggies because they believed everything we had to sell we stole. He told me it was a waste of time. Yes, in a way he was right, some people might not buy from us, either because they were too cheap, or because they wouldn't buy from druggies, but what about the tired ones or those too scared to ever go out into the bush?

Maybe someone will come to gather wood tomorrow and find me here. Maybe they'll help me get out of this place. Or maybe they'll be too scared and leave me tied up to this tree.

Toothless always told me we needed to keep the drag-on's stomach full, because then it wouldn't get angry and destroy everything in its path. Nothing can satisfy it but its main course—meth. Nothing makes sense to you when it's hungry. All that matters is the next hit. Yes, it was wrong to steal Nique's cellphone, but what else can you do if you need to feed the animal inside of you? Nique would never understand. She doesn't know what the dragon's like when it gets hungry. Even if I tried to explain, even if I tried to show her that I would never take from her again, she wouldn't understand.

Nique warned me from day one to stay away from Toothless, but I never listened. I miss Nique. She always gave me a second chance, even if she didn't understand me. Like when I saw her on Sunday at Byron's Shebeen. I'm glad she said something to Clint about the way he treats me, even if she doesn't understand my relationship with Clint. I don't like it when she visits Byron. She deserves better. I wanted to tell her that night that she should leave him. I wanted to tell her how Byron and his guards use me when there aren't any women around to satisfy them for the night. But I knew she wouldn't believe me. I wanted to tell her that, if she could help me, I would change my ways. But I didn't say anything. The dragon was growing hungrier and angrier, and Clint was taking his time giving me something to quiet the hunger. But what would it have mattered? I know she doesn't believe in me anymore. Clint said he can't understand how a man who has a wife and kids could fall in love with a make-believe woman. I asked him what he meant because Nique wasn't make-believe. I told him she's a woman. Clint asked me if Jesus made her a woman. The look he gave me told me that it wasn't a question that I needed to answer.

I told Toothless that we should wait for Clint, since he owed me money. But Toothless wanted to know if I was crazy because he needed to smoke. I tried explaining again, but when the dragon starts roaring inside of Toothless, he can't hear anything else, so I kept quiet. His jaw was doing the dance, his eyes darting all over because his next hit was just a glimpse away. I thought of the half straw in my pocket that Clint gave me. I thought maybe I should just give it to him so he could silence the dragon for a bit, but I knew he would freak out on me for not telling him sooner. His bite was worse than his bark.

While we walked down Hope Street, I tried to joke with him, but he just looked at me like I swore at his mother. Toothless has a short fuse, even when his dragon is fed. I tried getting him a job with Clint, but on his first night working with us he got into a fight with one of the other guards. I asked Toothless if he had a plan for how we were going to dodge the security guards at the train yard. He said nothing, just whistled and smiled to himself. Toothless used to have dentures in place of his four front teeth. The dentures were made up of two gold teeth and two teeth with gold tips, but he pawned them a long time ago. I once asked him where his name Toothless came from. He told me to go suck on my mother because it wasn't my business. But then I looked at him, and I understood. He had lost most of his teeth, he had a bald spot in the middle of his head with the clumps of hair standing up like a dragon's horns on either side, and his cheekbones looked like they were on the verge of breaking through his skin. Pimples lived rent free on his cheeks. He was stupid to sell the one thing that made him look better, but what can a person do when they have a need to fill? When your dragon roars, you have to listen.

Toothless boasted that he knew one of the security guards working at the train yard that night. His brother's friend. But I knew that Toothless and his brother didn't like each other. He warned me if I didn't stop nagging him about it all then I should just turn around and fuck off back home. When he said that, I told myself to turn around, but my dragon was in the driver's seat. I knew the half a straw in my pocket wouldn't get me through the night, so I kept quiet and continued walking with him. He reminded me again just how useless I was and told me that the only person he could ever depend on was Lentie, his ex. He bragged that she would help him without talking back or questioning everything he told her to do. I don't like that bitch, and I just wanted to show Toothless that he can depend on me. I wanted to show him that I'm better than her, that I work for what I want.

Lentie always appeared just when we started smoking. It was like she always knew just when we were about to smoke, then she showed up. And she stayed 'til we'd smoked up everything, and then disappeared to the next spot where she went to sell her body for a hit or two. She never had any money to add. Lentie, she's just like my sister, always waiting on their children's grants to come through, and when they get that money, then they're nowhere to be found. She's the one making up stories and telling people that Toothless fucks me whenever he wants, but that's not true. I'm not a whore like she is. She told everyone who would listen that I lay on my back for Toothless, and the more she told the story, the more imaginative it got. I almost fucked her up the day she told me men can't suck off other men. She told me the devil is my father. I told her to occupy herself with the shit she catches on before she talks about other people. But it's not like she cared about that because talking shit about other people is her hobby. That day she almost lost her dentures because of the stories she made up. Even Toothless agreed with me.

We continued walking in silence 'til we got to Toothless's granny's house. He told me to wait outside. It wasn't long before his brother started screaming at the top of his lungs that Toothless needed to fuck off out of the house. I could hear Toothless's granny tell his brother to leave Toothless alone. I always knew that Toothless could do no wrong in his granny's eyes and that she always stood up for him, but that day I saw it with my own eyes. It wasn't long before Toothless walked out of his granny's yard with a shopping cart and we left.

I told Toothless that the cops would pick us up if they found us walking around with a shopping cart that wasn't supposed to be in our possession. He told me that I should shut up and help him push the cart. I told him the cops wouldn't care where we found it, they would just pick us up because they felt like it. He told me to shut up and push. I could see someone had tried scraping the store name off the handle of the shopping cart, but the red-and-yellow logo known to everyone in the Shadows was still peeking through. Whoever it was that tried scraping it off was really stupid, because even if they were able to scrape the brand name off the handle, the cops would still know where we stole it from because there is only one big supermarket in the Shadows and that's Shoprite.

Clint told me about how Toothless had tried pawning his brother's big-screen TV at Byron's. It's no wonder his brother fucked him up the other day. Clint said Toothless was probably too embarrassed to tell me why he was sleeping on an old couch behind his granny's house. If my sister and her ass of a boyfriend were better people, I would've told Toothless to stay with us. I have enough space in my room for an extra single mattress. But maybe it's a good thing I can use my sister and her boyfriend as an excuse because sometimes it seems like Toothless has more than just the dragon to deal with. But just imagine what it must be like to live like a dog, outside under the moon and stars, in the wind and rain.

On our way to the train yard I saw Sara. She was coming out of the shop on the corner of her street. She was with Rosco, and they were all lovey-dovey with each other. They couldn't stop looking into each other's eyes. She didn't even see me waving. I wanted to stop to say hello, but Toothless started walking faster, like we were late for something, dragging me along behind the shopping cart. The sun was setting. That's probably why he was in such a hurry. Now that I think about it, maybe he knew something I didn't. Or maybe the dragon's hunger is just making me think crazy thoughts, because how could Toothless have known to wait for me on that corner? How could he know that I would go to Nique's house? How could he know about the people in the bush?

I wish they had tied me closer to the fire, but it's like they've forgotten I'm here. Before they covered my head, I tried shouting to the hooded one standing closest to me but that pillowcase-head just ignored me and continued focusing on the people dancing and chanting around the fire. It's not like this is my first time spending a night outside, but at least the last time my dragon was quiet.

A few weeks ago, my sister went to our cousin's for the weekend. Her boyfriend stayed at home and acted like I was the one who was a guest in my mother's house. I helped Clint and Byron with a shipment. First, we carried it into the lab inside the house, then they cut it with whatever they were cutting it with, and then we loaded it back into the van. Clint then took it to their stash house. I don't know where that is. No one knows, except Clint. He always drops me off before driving away with the drugs in the back of the van. I once told him that I wouldn't mind helping offload the drugs, but he just laughed and said he'd have to kill me when we were done with the job. But I think I know where he stashes it. His baby's mama lives a few streets away from me. I guess Clint was right not to trust a druggie, but I'm not like Toothless and Pete. I never asked to help him again because I don't want to die yet. Life is still good, at least sometimes. Other times I have to get on all fours in front of Byron and Clint and they do whatever they want with me. That night was one of those times.

It normally happens on Byron's and Clint's days off when they're at the shebeen drinking, drugging, and fucking everyone around them. Last time it happened there were about twenty girls laying around, being fucked by all the guards one after the other. But sometimes there aren't enough girls to go around, or Byron wants a different taste in his mouth, or the girls are too high or drunk, so Byron smacks them around before he signals me to come over.

It was a late autumn night a few weeks back. The air was cold, filled with the promise of rain. As usual, there were lots of drunk and drugged-up girls at the disposal of Byron and his army of men. But Byron got angry at one of the girls trying to suck him off in the back of the shebeen. The lights were dim, but anyone could see everything play out in detail. Byron scolded Clint for bringing pieces of shit into his home. Clint said nothing back and grabbed the girl by her arm. He told me to help him carry all the girls out, but before we could take them, Byron started feeling sorry for them and told us to stop and leave them where they were. Both of us knew that was not the reason why Byron told us to leave them where they were. Everyone talks about the rapes that happen at Byron's Shebeen. How he has illegitimate kids all across the Shadows. And the stories go that it doesn't matter how fucked-up the girls are, Byron will have his way with them and allow his bouncers to do the same.

I'm still trying to understand why he has such a hold over Nique, because it's not like she doesn't know about the things that happen at the shebeen. Nique has never used anything in her life other than alcohol. She keeps to her cider, most of the time.

She told me one night when we were still in high school that she was in love with me. She was drunk. Both of us were drunk. I acted silly and laughed. After all, she was one of my best friends and, really, the only one who cared about me after my mother's passing. Why would you fuck up a friendship with sex? I don't know what she sees in that pig. Byron does what he wants, when he wants, to whoever he wants. I don't know why I never told her about his bullshit. Maybe she could've taken me away from there. Maybe I wouldn't be sitting here now in my own piss and shit, tied up to a tree.

That night Byron signaled me over. He told Clint to fetch a case of beer, but to take his time with it. Clint and I both knew what that meant because Byron only drinks gin, and the beer drinkers were all passed out on the couches and floor of the shebeen. Half-naked bodies looked like cheap confetti strewn after a budget wedding. Clint says Byron drinks gin to keep him sober enough to remember the shit he does.

Byron sat on his throne, a red couch in the middle of the back wall of the shebeen. He unbuttoned his jeans, pulled out his hard dick, and leaned back. That was my cue. I slowly walked over to him. Sometimes I can see why Nique finds him attractive. There's something about the scars on his square face, his thick nose, and his big lips threatening to burst at the seams that speaks to the beauty in ugliness. His red throne complemented the dark shimmer of his skin. One hand was lying on the armrest and the other was slowly massaging his dick. Eyes closed, soft moans escaping with his every exhale. I knelt in front of him and wondered if I'd ever get a chance to be a king like him, but a better one, not like the don, but different, kinder to everyone.

When I touched him, his free hand connected with the side of my face. "Warm up your fucking hands," he threatened.

Every time I had to kneel to put my lips around Byron's dick, I wished I had the guts to kill him right there, to take his throne right in that moment. Then Nique would be rid of him, then the Shadows would be rid of him, and I could be a better ruler to everyone. But I could never silence the fear of not being able to feed my dragon whenever I needed to. Byron's Shebeen was where I could always find my dragon's next meal without having to go to too much trouble. There was always a dick waiting to be drained.

When Byron's dick was limp in my mouth, he told me to fuck off. And, like usual, Clint was waiting for me outside, with my money for the night and his load ready. I know he watched while Byron was busy with me. I always wished Byron and Clint would get together so we wouldn't have to suffer under their hands. But neither one wanted to feel like the bitch; both wanted to be the pimp.

It's Clint's eyes that scare me most. The smirk lingering in his eyes when Byron throws a fist through a girl's face. It's almost like he enjoys other people's suffering. Like that night Byron dragged a girl who stole from him into his house by her hair. Clint's eyes reminded me of Mandy's when Mom or Dad brought us something nice.

Clint never likes me to look at him. So he told me to face the wall. I let my pants and underwear fall to the floor. The cold played over my ass cheeks. Clint pushed me up against the wall. I'm never allowed to touch him either. I heard the rip of his teeth tearing into the condom wrapper. His breathing was louder than usual, like he was getting more excited. I was glad it didn't take long. I longed for my bed, not knowing what was waiting for me at home.

That night Clint dropped me off in front of my house. The doors were locked, and the spare keys weren't in their usual spot. I shouted for Mandy's boyfriend to open the door, but he never came. I thought about walking back to Byron's Shebeen, but it was too far. That wasn't the first time I slept outside, but this time it wasn't by choice. I could deal with the cold; the dragon provided me with some heat. I made a small fire in the corner of the backyard closest to my sister's bedroom window, hoping the smoke would wake Mandy's boyfriend from his fake sleep. I took the bath towel he forgot outside on the washing line and threw it down on the ground to give me some protection against the wet black earth. I knew he would be pissed, but I didn't care.

The cruelest thing about that night wasn't the fact that I slept outside, or the abuse I got from Byron or Clint, but the longing I had in my heart for my dead mother. When I smoke, her memory grows bigger and bigger with every exhale, but then she disappears like childhood happiness. So the more I miss her, the more I smoke, hoping that the next hit will bring her back forever. With every pull on the meth pipe, I feel her come to life. And the Red Door perfume she loved dances on my skin.

It was cold that night, but Mom was there sitting next to that fire with me. But tonight I can't feel her. Maybe if I explained this to Nique, she would understand. I don't smoke to forget, but to remember. Because when I smoke Mom is back here with me.

6

A HOUSE WITHOUT A MOTHER

Tuesday

I t was Tuesday morning, and Gershwin felt grateful for the silence that came with being awake so early. Despite the chilly winter air clawing through his bedroom window, he preferred to keep it open for the crisp breeze. He moved his chair closer to the window and pushed it farther ajar. His grandma Johanna Lawrence had taught him a lot, and waking up early in the mornings was one of those lessons. He remembered how he would wake up next to his grandma, who was sitting in bed, one hand holding a cup of tea, the other holding her small blue Bible, reading softly to herself. He never said anything; he just lay next to her, eyes closed and ears wide open, listening to his grandma quietly reading Psalms to herself. He saw the jealousy in his mother's eyes because his grandma chose him over his mother to sleep next to her in her double bed. He could never understand why his mother hated his grandmother so much.

Most of the time he felt like he was not his mother's child. The money he gave her was never enough. Sometimes he didn't know what she even did with the money, but he just kept on giving her more. Even though his grandma raised him with the Bible always close by, his mother was pushing him further away from it. He blamed the Bible for the way his mother treated him. She believed every word of it and every day was trying to push it down everyone's throat. His grandma never did that. She had always loved Jesus in her own way. She was a good person with a good heart. She never once raised her voice to him. She never made him feel that he wasn't enough. He knew his mother didn't care about him, but sometimes he wished that she could be different. Sometimes he missed having a relationship like Sara had with her mother, but he knew his mother would never change.

Gershwin heard a noise outside in the street, but it wasn't his neighbour's dog barking and playing with its empty water bowl in the dark like he'd heard earlier. He got up and pushed the window wide enough to lean his whole upper body through. He looked out into the dimly lit street to try to identify where the noise was coming from. The only thing he could discern in the blurry beams of the streetlight was the gentle, misty rain that had started to fall like dust, without a sound. Gershwin held his breath for a few seconds to give all his energy to his ears stretching out into the darkness of the street. That's when he heard the scraping sounds echoing down the street again, like something metal and heavy was being dragged over the asphalt. He recognized the noise from a few weeks back when he had seen Toothless and Carl walking down Hope Street together, deep in conversation, Toothless dragging a shopping cart half-full of scrap metal.

Gershwin hung out of the window as the rumbling noise came closer and closer. Finally, he saw Toothless and Pete pushing a shopping cart full of what he assumed was metal scraps again. They were the only ones desperate enough to get up to this shit this early in the morning. But he didn't see Carl this time. Gershwin closed his window and sat in front of his old desktop computer. Selling scraps looked like a lucrative business. *Maybe I should start doing that*, he thought, before going to make coffee.

LATER THAT MORNING, GERSHWIN heard his mother dragging her foot as she walked out of her bedroom into the bathroom. His grandma had told him how his mother had ended up under a minibus taxi. She had almost lost her legs. He sipped the last bit of his third coffee of the morning and waited until she was back in her bedroom before getting up to make more.

She's finally cleaned the kitchen, he thought. He wondered what Richard had thought of the sink full of dirty dishes. Gershwin switched on the kettle. The water slowly started singing as the kettle's element heated up. He was careful with all his movements. He knew his mother would have a fit thinking he would eat all the food. *I didn't eat last night*, he thought, rubbing his tummy. He opened the kitchen cupboard. The salt and pepper containers and one tin of baked beans stared back at him. He slammed the cupboard doors, not caring if his mother heard him. He searched the fridge, which didn't look more promising than the cupboard. The water bottles inside did nothing more than reiterate that there was no food in the house. Gershwin didn't understand what happened to the money he gave his mother. He started to storm down the short corridor to his mother's bedroom door but quickly turned and retraced his steps into the kitchen. It wasn't worth the fight.

He poured the last bit of coffee and sugar into his mug and took it back to his bedroom. He knew he had lost the fight with his mother even before it started. *No bread, no food, and Lord knows what she does with the soap*, he thought. Gershwin decided not to collect another food parcel at the community hall. He was tired of his mother hiding it all in her bedroom cupboard. He put his mug down on his desk and looked at the photo of his granny hanging on his bedroom wall. He knew that she looked over him, even if only from the photo.

Gershwin locked his bedroom door, rolled up the bath towel hanging over his clothing cupboard's door, and pushed it into the space between the floor and the door to keep his cigarette smoke from seeping into the rest of the house. He knew he could just pack up and leave. He didn't have an excuse not to move in with Nique with all the money he'd saved up. He reached for the small shoebox behind the row of bigger shoe-boxes in his cupboard. He knew he had to deposit the money before someone broke in and stole it, or before his mother got a hold of it.

Gershwin continued working through the morning, troubleshooting an old laptop a neighbour had asked him to fix. He decided to keep the loaf of bread he'd bought in his room. He packed most of his clothes and shoes in the suitcase he kept next to his cupboard and stuffed the half-full bag between the wall and the cupboard. He'd have enough time to move out at the end of the week when his mother was at church.

Gershwin listened to his mother's angry movements in the kitchen as she banged one kitchen cupboard door after the other. Then Rose banged on his bedroom door when she realized it was locked. "Open this fucking door!" she screamed.

Gershwin waited for his mother to stop banging before he opened the door. "Why must you go on like this?"

"Why must I beg you to let me into a room in my own house?" she shouted back. "And why did you drink up all the coffee?"

"If you didn't go to church so much, people would say that you're on drugs or something."

"Drugs? Me?" Rose stood with her hands on her hips.

"Who gives you the right to speak to me like this? Last I checked you are living under my roof."

"Excuse me?" Gershwin knew that his daily fight with his mother had started, and he had a choice to either take part in it or get himself ready for his day. "Is this your house? Mom, did you forget what your mother told you? What my granny said?"

His mother walked away in silence back to the kitchen, defeated.

"Yeah, now you have nothing to say because you know the truth. This is not your house alone," said Gershwin. "It's my house just as much as it's yours. That's what Granny said. So deal with it!" he yelled after her.

The flickering red light on his cellphone grabbed his attention. He read the WhatsApp message from Sara. He tapped and held the little microphone in the right-hand corner of the cellphone's screen and said, "What do you mean? No, I haven't seen Carl. I told you I last saw him a week ago." He waited a few seconds to see if she would respond to his voice note but then pushed the cellphone back in his pocket. He saw his mother pass his open bedroom door carrying the coffee and sugar containers back to the kitchen. He got up and followed her and gasped when he saw both containers were filled up.

"So this whole time you had coffee and sugar in your bedroom, but then you turn around and shout at me about there not being any food?" Gershwin said, outraged.

His mother said nothing and placed the containers back in the cupboard. Gershwin went back to his bedroom

83

and flung the door closed, but didn't bother to lock it. He pulled a cigarette from the packet on his desk and threw his cellphone next to his computer. He grabbed his cellphone when a message alert came through. Gershwin listened to Sara say, "I'm just checking in. Maybe he's next door with Toothless?"

Gershwin sent Sara another voice note. "Girl, you will never get the real story from Toothless. Can you believe it, early this morning, him and Pete were out and about dragging a shopping cart full of scraps down the street. Now you know they'll be smoking for the entire day, so I'm not gonna waste my time even asking them."

Next he read a message from Nique reminding him to call a new client who needed his computer fixed. Gershwin sent a voice note asking, "Nique, where are you? Have you heard anything from Carl yet?" But it took too long to upload. Gershwin cursed the slow internet the community had been experiencing. He threw his cellphone back on his desk and squashed his cigarette butt in an ashtray. He pulled another cigarette from the pack lying on his desk and held the lighter up toward the light coming through his window to see how much gas was left before he brought the yellow flame to the tip. His eyes jumped from the door to the cellphone's screen. He sighed with relief when he saw that Nique had finally heard his message.

"Morning!" Nique's voice sang over the voice note. "I haven't heard or seen him, but you know how Carl is. He's here today, gone tomorrow. So I wouldn't worry too much about it. He's probably locked up behind the doors of one of those meth houses down on Mandela Street." Gershwin moved from his desk to his bed, still sucking on the cigarette. Despite what Nique said, he knew that she was worried about Carl. He sent Sara yet another voice note. "Sara, Nique said we have nothing to worry about, but I could hear it in her voice that she's worried about him."

Gershwin pulled his hair into a bun with a hair clip from the small box next to his makeup bag. His cell-phone's screen flickered, but he ignored it and continued doing his hair. The phone flickered for a second time. He sighed, picked it up, and saw an unknown number flashing on the screen. *It must be a new client*, he thought, *someone Nique gave my number to.*

"Gershwin Computers, how can I help you?" he said. He knew his granny would be proud of his business. He was not sure that she would be happy about the other services he offered only to his male clients. He knew she wouldn't accept it, but what choice did he have? He needed more money. When he had started his business, he had realized how easy it was to meet men who felt neglected and alone, under the guise of fixing their laptops or computers. Gershwin loved his job servicing computers and their owners.

"Yes, hi. You're speaking to him. How can I help you? Oh…yes…" Gershwin flipped open the hardcover exercise book he used for work. "I have a Windows upgrade for you, yes. No worries, I'll do it for you tomorrow, Mrs.

Pietersen," said Gershwin. "Thank you, Mrs. Pietersen. I know where you live." He lit another cigarette while listening to his new client. "No, sorry, Mrs. Pietersen. It's cash on delivery. Okay, see you tomorrow. Bye." *She's trying her luck*, he thought. More than a few people had conned Gershwin into fixing their computers and then not paid him for the work he'd done. *People will sell their souls just to get something for free*, he thought.

A shadow fell through Gershwin's window frame. He looked up and saw his friend Nique standing there smiling.

"Thanks for the mini heart attack," said Gershwin.

"Girl, we need to do something about that thing on your head," said Nique, leaning on the sill. "No, queen, that 'do won't do you any good." She laughed. She pulled a square tampon tin full of her hairstyling tools out of the bag over her shoulder.

"Where did you come from?" asked Gershwin.

Nique's hand scrabbled in her bag and pulled out her cellphone.

"So I'm talking to myself now?" said Gershwin. "Or you just don't want to tell me who you were with?"

"Looks like someone got up on the wrong side of the bed," said Nique with a smirk.

"You've got time for jokes? You know too well there's only one side to my bed." Gershwin laughed. "It's the devil herself. She knows just how to fuck up my day."

"Oh my god, friend," said Nique. "You need to get out of here. But first let's do something with that little monster you call your hair."

86

"No, not today. You know these walls are thin, and it's hard to keep you quiet. I really don't have the energy for my mother's bullshit," said Gershwin. "And the two of you are reactive. Oil and water much? So if you're gonna come in, please be a ghost."

"You know she's only hating because she's the biggest lesbian in town. No one who's certain of their sexuality would act the way she's acting," said Nique. "I wonder what her face would look like if she found out about you and her darling pastor."

"Shhh—wait, what do you mean?" said Gershwin.

"Do you think I don't know what happens on your visits with the pastor?" asked Nique. "It's weird that she doesn't know. I mean, her only son is the biggest queen in the Shadows. I don't think your mother's gonna think it's funny that you're keeping her crush warm."

"Nique, stop talking nonsense," said Gershwin. "Please, people around here think they know what's going on, but do they really? And you, ma'am, I think you need to be more worried about your weekly dates at Byron's Shebeen."

"Wow, you two should get Oscars for your performances. Your mom playing the holiest of church sisters and you playing the straightest man living in the Shadows. Bravo, that's all I have to say," Nique said, trying to deflect attention away from her and Byron.

"You know, sometimes you really talk shit. Just come in and don't make any noise," said Gershwin. "But wait, what do you mean she's playing a role?"

Nique laughed at the confused frown on Gershwin's face. "It's nothing, don't worry about it," said Nique. "Just open the door." She took another drag from her cigarette and threw the burning butt under her shoe. Her hand dug in her bag again, and after a few seconds she pulled out pink lip gloss. "I'm tired of walking all over the place." She sighed. "I think it's time for a car, what do you think?"

"Good idea. Buy a car and take me far away from here because my tired is tired," said Gershwin. "Can you believe there is nothing to eat in this house? I don't know what my mother does with the money I give her."

"Gershwin, have you ever asked her what she does with the money?"

"Do you know something I don't?"

"No, I'm just asking," said Nique. "Can you please stop asking questions and come open the door for me?"

"Now I know you're hiding something from me," said Gershwin. "I've known you for far too long and too well to know that you're not telling me everything. And I know it's about my mother and something she did. So you can just come out and tell me."

"Yeah, it's kind of like you hiding a Pastor Richard–sized secret in your pants," Nique joked, and walked off before Gershwin could interrogate her any further.

Nique went around the back of the house to the kitchen door, where she saw Toothless next door sitting legs spread apart on a broken shopping cart turned on its side.

"Hey, sexy, how about you and me, naked on your

double bed?" Toothless laughed, taking a makeshift pipe from Pete made from the neck of a broken beer bottle and the silver liner from a cigarette pack.

"Just focus on smoking your pipe and continuing your fantasy, but leave me out of it," said Nique, waiting for Gershwin to open the weathered kitchen door.

"He's just giving you a compliment, girl," said Pete, who was balancing on a three-legged garden chair held up by two cement blocks.

Nique turned away as Toothless tried his best to help Pete light the marijuana mixed with Mandrax in the pipe. Pete sucked hard, his cheeks inflating and deflating as he tried to ignite the pipe. It didn't take long. The flames climbed up the insides of the pipe. Pete's body heaved with every inhalation, and the smoke left behind with every pull bubbled out of his mouth. A few moments passed before he pushed the smoke in his lungs out through his nostrils. His body weakened. All his movements slowed down. Even when he fell, it was in slow motion, rocking forward then backward, then sliding down against the trunk of the tree behind him.

Toothless grabbed the pipe from his friend's hand and took the same path. The pipe fell from his hands as the drugs swam through his bloodstream and his body drooped. He leaned back, searching for the security of a chair that wasn't there, forgetting where he was and what he was sitting on. Nique laughed at Toothless lying on the ground with his legs dangled over the flipped shopping cart.

"That'll teach you to mess with grown-ups." Nique laughed. She tried the kitchen door, which was unlocked. She walked in and her eyes wandered across the kitchen floor, kettle, and microwave that had aged from white to yellow with time. The kitchen sink was half filled with water with two dish towels soaking in it, emanating a powerful bleach smell.

Gershwin flung his bedroom door open and ran into the kitchen. His voice made a weird screeching sound as he whispered frantically. "I told you my mother is home. I could hear your every move through my door," he said. "Why do you bother with those guys? Then you're in the street shouting at them? You just don't care about no one, do you?" Gershwin dragged Nique into his room and locked the door.

Nique threw herself on Gershwin's bed and made herself comfortable. She pulled out a cigarette, but Gershwin grabbed it out of her mouth before she could light it.

"What now?" asked Nique. "You bite my head off and tell me to keep quiet, and I did that. What did I do wrong now?"

"Oh, so you want me dead?" asked Gershwin, throwing the unlit cigarette on the bed next to Nique. "If my mother..."

"Oh, you're so dramatic," Nique said, chuckling at Gershwin who'd stopped talking with his hand on the side of his neck, his face scrunched up. "I think you missed your calling, my friend. You need to be onstage, Madam

90

Drama Queen. And another thing, do you think your mother can't smell the smoke that's already in here? Yes, girl, your theatrics need a stage." Nique laughed some more.

Gershwin finally joined in Nique's laughter and relaxed into a chair. "You think this is a joke? She will kill you with her bare hands, and then I'll be without a Nique," he said. "She really believes that you are the devil's work and that it's her duty to do God's work. She and Pastor Richard are on a mission to rid the Shadows of all evil..."

"Yes, but she's the biggest evil of them all," said Nique.

Gershwin got up and pushed the bath towel into the gap between the bedroom door and the floor. "She can't stop talking about the work their church does," he said.

"You're really not gonna offer me anything to drink?" asked Nique.

"Sorry, love, but even the coffee grounds are counted in this house." Gershwin laughed, sitting down next to Nique on the bed. "Earlier she filled up the sugar and coffee tins in her room."

"Wow, she's something else," said Nique, watching Gershwin tapping a pack of cigarettes against the side of his hand. "You need to stop smoking!"

"I could say the same thing to you," said Gershwin, lifting a lighter to his cigarette. "Shhh... What was that? Shut up!"

"What? It's not your mom. You would've heard her, Gersh," said Nique. "No one can live like this. When are you moving?"

"Sunday!" said Gershwin.

"Are you serious?" Nique threw her arms around Gershwin's shoulders and pulled him toward her. "I am so happy that you're finally moving out of hell."

"I just can't live like this anymore," said Gershwin. "See for yourself. I've already started packing." He pointed at the big suitcase pushed in between his cupboard and the wall. Nique was opening her mouth to reply when they heard Rose's door creaking.

"Gershwin, why do you have to make so much noise?" Rose complained. "How many times have I told you— my house, my rules. And before you start with that shit your grandma said, I don't care!" Gershwin's door handle jumped up and down as Rose tried to get in. "What did I tell you about locked doors in my house? What are you up to in there? Open this bloody door!" she shouted.

"What about my privacy?" Gershwin shouted at his locked bedroom door.

"Privacy? Privacy! If you're looking for privacy, then go and look for it elsewhere. Because if I've told you once, I've told you a thousand times—no locked doors in my house!" screamed Rose. "And what did I tell you about smoking? Not in this house! Do you hear me?"

"I'm really sorry, my sister," said Gershwin, trying to stop himself from laughing. "How am I going to get you out of here? The window is a little small for you to get through, and my mother won't return to her room until later today. I'll keep her busy, but you'll need to find some wings and fly out that window. Fly, my sister, fly!"

"My god, we're not kids anymore," said Nique, louder than she needed to.

"Please!" begged Gershwin. "I'll make it up to you. Just please be quiet and wait for me to start fighting with her. That's the best distraction I can give you for your big escape."

"You'll follow the rules in God's house. Locked doors, smoking inside, and all this noise? When can I get some rest?" Rose screamed at Gershwin as he unlocked his door.

"I don't know why you have to go on like this." Gershwin sighed.

"You think fifty rand here and there is enough money for you to have a say in this house?" said Rose, dragging one of the kitchen chairs to the back door. She opened the top half of the door before she plumped herself down into the chair.

Gershwin pulled a mug out of the kitchen cupboard and poured in two heaped teaspoons of instant coffee. He pushed down the urge to make himself another cup of coffee. He didn't want to continue the battle with his mother, and he hoped making her a coffee would be distraction enough for Nique to escape.

"Why were you making so much noise in your room?" asked Rose. "That's what you want to do the entire day, sit in front of a computer, watch movies, and listen to music? When are you gonna get yourself a decent job?"

Gershwin placed the mug in his mother's hand when he heard a loud thud in his room. Frozen in fear that his mother had heard it, too, he looked at her, but her focus was on Toothless and Pete next door, still sitting under the tree in a drug-induced daze. Gershwin swung open the fridge door, knowing his action would pull his mother's gaze. He frowned at the empty shelves.

"Why must you fight about everything?" she asked.

Gershwin ignored her and pulled out the last pack of sausages from the freezer. "This is all that's left." He sighed. "What will we eat tomorrow?" Another thud came from his bedroom as Nique fell against Gershwin's cupboard trying to lift one leg through the window.

"What's wrong with you? Go and fetch my cigarettes!" Rose ordered.

Gershwin pulled a pack of cigarettes from one of the drawers in the kitchen cupboard and gave it to her. Confusion played on his face as he wondered how she failed to hear the noises coming from his room. She must be going deaf.

"Please, just leave me alone!" said Gershwin. He backed away from his mother as she moaned about his inability to make her a decent cup of coffee. When he opened his bedroom door, he expected to see Nique dangling through the window, but there was no sign of her. He locked his door again and shoved the towel back in its place.

"Sorry, Nique," he said to himself, and pulled a new pack of cigarettes out of one of the desk drawers. He sucked hard on the cigarette dangling between his lips. *That's the last time she'll speak to me like that*, he thought. *It's not how a mother should act.*

Gershwin finished his smoke. He grabbed his toiletries to go get ready for the day. He went to the bathroom where he placed a grey plastic basin inside the bathtub and filled it with warm water. Sitting on the side of the tub, he played with the water pouring out of the tap. Gershwin longed for a future where he didn't need to be scared or worried about living his life. A life where he didn't need to worry about constantly battling with his mother about things he didn't understand.

Gershwin turned off the water and moved the plastic basin to the centre of the bathtub. He threw a small torn hand towel in front of the bathtub and swung one leg after the other into the tub. Gershwin picked up his wash rag and a piece of soap and pushed both into the lukewarm water. His eyes grew soft as he drifted off into the past. He thought of the time when his granny was still alive. How she always made sure he was okay. He remembered the creases that showed the years on her face, her inviting smile. He thought of his mother, who could never seem to see him as her own. He had never felt her motherly love. He thought of his daily duties as a child and remembered how happy he was filling up the bath basin with a kettle of boiled water, lowering the temperature with cold tap water, and later throwing the used water out. It made him feel like he had a purpose. He remembered how his granny scolded him when some of the water spilled over the basin's edge, but her scolding came from a place of love, not hate. He remembered the fresh, herby smell that would waft up at him every morning when he threw the bathwater over his granny's plants.

Gershwin stood up with both his feet in the basin. He soaped his wash rag with rose-scented soap and started washing his upper body. He scrubbed harder than he normally would, almost like he was trying to rub the craziness of his mother off his body. After he washed his upper body, he filled a plastic jug with water from the basin and poured it over his shoulders. His shoulders relaxed as the lukewarm water rained down on them.

Gershwin picked up a pink disposable razor but then threw it back in his toiletries bag. He thought about the conversation he'd overheard between his mother and Pastor Richard the day before. He knew they were whispering about things that weren't for anyone else's ears. His face lit up as he thought of Pastor Richard's rusty voice that could always calm him down, but the darkness returned when he thought of his mother constantly trying to break his spirit.

As he got out of the bathtub to use the toilet, Gershwin caught his reflection in the mirror. His cheeks flamed up as he thought of his last session with Pastor Richard, but his daydream was stopped in its tracks by his mother shouting, "Who do you think's gonna cook dinner tonight? Finish up in there and go and drop off the thumb drive with the pastor's music so you can come back and cook."

Gershwin was annoyed but smiled at the thought of seeing Pastor Richard. He picked up the pink razor again and placed a towel on the edge of the bathtub. He stepped back into the tub and picked up the soap to wash the rest of his body.

"Did you hear me?" his mother asked.

"I'm almost done!" he shouted. His reflection looked at him. He poured another jug of water over his head. In the summer when they were in high school, he and Carl would chase each other with buckets of cold water. Gershwin couldn't remember where they got the buckets, but he remembered Carl's joy-filled screams, his bushy eyebrows against his brown skin, and how his veins would push up against his skin, a sign that his heart was pumping harder than usual. He remembered how Carl's top lip would always flip up when he spoke.

Gershwin's eyes travelled over his stomach, following his wash rag in his hands. He remembered the day he stopped caring about Carl. It was raining and Carl was standing on the corner of Hope and Main, his head on a swivel as he searched for his next hit. Gershwin had crossed the road, head down, eyes glued to the ground before Carl could see him. Now Gershwin felt shame run hot over his cheeks. For giving up on his friend, telling himself and anyone who would listen that Carl didn't want to be helped. He felt ashamed for giving up on Carl, but how can you help someone who refuses anyone's help?

Banging on the bathroom door had him scrambling out of the bathtub. He grabbed the two towels he had brought into the bathroom with him and wrapped one around his body and the other around his wet hair. He pushed all his toiletries into the bag and tugged lightly on the towel around his body to make sure it was secure before he unlocked the door. He turned around to check that he had all his belongings and everything was in its place. A slight breeze opened the door. The broken lock, close to falling out, was not strong enough to keep the door shut. As Gershwin walked out, he almost bumped into his mother, who was standing with her hands on her hips waiting for him.

"Is that how a man uses a towel?" asked Rose.

Gershwin shrank away and used his arms as a barrier between him and his mother as she tried to pull the towel off his head. Her second attempt was successful, and she threw the towel in his face.

"There's something really wrong with you," he said. He laughed darkly and walked into his bedroom.

"Go ahead, laugh all you want. Laugh! No child of mine is a faggot. No child of mine! Do you hear me!" she screamed. "Don't let me see that shit again! Not in this fucking house. Not under my roof! You hear me?

Gershwin slammed his bedroom door and locked it. He ignored his mother's screams and pulled a T-shirt over his head. He picked up the black skinny jeans hanging off his bed and slipped into them without putting any underwear on. Looking in the mirror hanging on the door of his clothing cupboard, he traced the dark shadows forming under his eyes with his finger. *You're gonna die here*, he thought.

7

THE TRAIL

Last Wednesday

This is the third day of being tied up to a tree. When I met Toothless on the corner it was like any other Monday afternoon for me. Kids were playing in the streets, minibus taxis snaked through the Shadows, making rhythmic stops as they dropped off people coming home from their jobs. Toothless pulled the front of the shopping cart, and I pushed from the back. After sunset we reached the stream running around the Shadows and took Hope Street. Then we followed the train tracks 'til we reached the canal. The water was low enough for us to cross, but the current was strong. Everywhere the water created its own pathways over broken beer bottles and other rubbish. On the other side of the canal bank a plastic garden table lay upside down, three legs in the air. Parts of the white plastic had turned a brownish green.

I tried making conversation with Toothless, but all I got was him telling me to stop talking shit and do my job. But I didn't feel bad at all because that was just Toothless. So I followed him without saying anything more. Toothless didn't see a small pile of rubbish in front of him and tripped. I tried to keep the shopping cart upright, but Toothless pulled it after him. His left knee hit the water first, then came the rest of him. He reminded me of Pete's dog shivering outside in the rain, and I laughed. He grabbed the first thing he could get his hands on and threw it at me. I tried getting out of the way, but the piece of slimy plastic shopping bag landed on my chest. I had to listen again to how useless I was. I decided not to tell him how he was the one that fell and not me. He was the one who didn't look where he was going.

We picked up the shopping cart in silence, with Toothless still brushing mud and trash off his clothes. When we reached the other side of the shallow canal, Toothless moved to the back of the cart and indicated with his eyes that I should take on his duties at the front. I asked him why we didn't take the easier route over the train bridge because it crosses over the canal. The anger in his stare told me to shut up, but I wondered how we would be able to push the shopping cart through the thick bush, with overgrown trees and roots sticking out of the ground. Toothless eventually told me that we'd use the bridge when we came back. I didn't think I wouldn't see the bridge that night. A few metres from the bank of the canal we pushed the empty shopping cart down a bush trail, making our way to the scrapyard.

It wasn't long before we heard the singing. Toothless stopped pushing and just stared at me with anxiety growing bigger in his eyes. It was the first time I saw him scared. I didn't understand why he looked so afraid. I asked him if someone had started a church in the bush, but he didn't answer me. I asked him who he thought it could be. In return, he asked me if he had X-ray vision to see through the bushes. He told me that we should leave the shopping cart and follow a different bush trail toward the voices to see what was happening.

I was scared. I didn't want to walk in front. The bush was thick and the trail wasn't clear. Toothless directed my steps from behind, telling me to just go straight. Like he knew where to step. I followed his orders and did what he told me to do. I figured he came to the bush a lot and knew the trails better than I did. The singing grew louder, and that's when I saw the fire. The yellow flames winked at us through the trees and bushes. I couldn't understand what they were singing. Toothless kept on telling me not to worry, and that I should just continue walking straight. It was the first time that day that Toothless had a lot to say to me, but I kept my anger to myself and just did what he told me to do.

The trail became wider the closer we got to the singing and the fire. And then it made a right turn just before we stepped into a clearing in the bush. That's when I saw them. They reminded me of a movie I once saw of people dressed all in white, with their heads covered in white hoods, standing next to a burning cross. This scene looked the same, just without the cross. I told Toothless we should leave, but he told me I should shove my fear up my ass because they didn't know we were there. I asked him if they were traditional healers and if they worshipped God, because some of the hooded people were standing with what looked like Bibles in their hands. I remember one of them turned toward us, like they were expecting us, and that's when I saw that even their faces were covered, with holes cut out for their eyes.

I asked Toothless why we were going toward the people. He told me to stop asking questions and just walk. I asked him why we were leaving the shopping cart behind because we wouldn't be able to carry the metal scraps. He didn't change his tune and kept telling me to shut up and to walk straight. Before long I realized that the footsteps following me were not Toothless's anymore.

I took a second too long to start running. I couldn't see much in front of me, but I ran. I heard the footsteps storming toward me. I believed if I followed Toothless's directions that I would get away from the footsteps. Going straight was the last thing I thought about before a root took hold of my foot and sent me stumbling, then falling to the ground. Branches slipped through my fingers as I tried to catch myself. I screamed for Toothless to help me, but he was gone. There was only a sharp knee drilling into my back, pushing the last little bit of air out of my lungs. I couldn't breathe. I pushed up, trying to get out from under the weight stabbing into my back, but it was too heavy. And the harder I tried, the harder the person pushed a knee into my back and a hand on the back of my head. I felt hands grabbing each of my arms. They pulled me to my feet. I shouted, pleading with Toothless for help, but one guy laughed and joked with one of the others that they had just been waiting for this delivery. What he said didn't make sense. I asked him what he meant.

"Your friend sold you for a few straws of meth."

I tried fighting, but they were too strong. I knew the guy was lying. Toothless would never do that to me. I tried shouting, but all I got was a bloody mouth and a loose tooth. They looked funny with their pillowcase-heads with crooked eyes and no mouths, but there was nothing funny about my situation. Their mouthless faces reminded me of the night Sara helped me scare Gershwin. We pulled Sara's mother's pillowcases over our heads and threw a white sheet over our shoulders. Gershwin didn't speak to us for the rest of the night.

Clint once told me about the devil worshippers that use the bush to do the things they can't do out in the open. I told him they would never dare to do these things in the Shadows because there are too many churches, and everyone knows everyone.

He told me about the things people had to do to join them. He said he didn't like the idea of drinking cat's blood. I told him his stories didn't scare me, and things like that only happened in the movies. But there was something in the way one of the pillowcase-heads looked at me that reminded me of Clint, and I remembered he always had a certain smell to him. Same as my mom always had a smell unique to her. I told the one who smelled like Clint that it was me, and begged him to help me, but they both just laughed and pulled the wire they tied around my arms tighter.

They didn't speak again. I told them I had done nothing wrong, and that they must let me go, but no one listened, or if they were listening, I wouldn't have known the difference. Without saying a word to each other, they strung me up between them and dragged me to a tree far away from the fire. Everything was in place. One end of a thick piece of wire was tied around the tree trunk, the other end was waiting for me. I was starting to believe that Toothless really had led me there. But why me? What did I do wrong?

They pushed me up against the trunk, and the cool ridges of the bark I felt on my back brought me some comfort. The one who smelled like Clint started walking around the tree with the other end of the piece of wire in his hand. With every circle he completed, the wire pulled tighter around my chest. I told them I couldn't breathe and begged them to stop. The ones standing around the fire turned their heads toward me all at the same time, and then in unison turned back to face the fire in front of them. It was like they didn't want to witness the lamb being tied up ready for slaughter. They stopped singing for a little bit, listening to the dance of the fire.

I tried telling them they had the wrong person, but they didn't budge. After I took Nique's cellphone, I never stole again, I told them, but still there was no response.

Then one of the others stepped away from the fire and came to stand right in front of me. It was a man. He grumbled for me to shut up. His voice was deep. I told him that I didn't steal anything. I told him that it was Toothless's idea to go look for scrap metal. But it was clear that no one would listen. With every order for me to shut up, this hooded man's voice got angrier.

One of them started recording on a cellphone. I told them I had to piss. The one who stood in front of me lifted a Bible toward me and whispered a prayer. It made no sense to me that people like this worshipped the same god my mother worshipped. I couldn't hold it in any longer and my piss formed a pool right where I was sitting. First I felt a warmth, and then a chill spread through my legs and my ass.

I thought of how Mandy would react if I didn't come home. When Mom passed, it was just the two of us looking out for one another. I begged them to let me go. I told them that my sister needed me. That didn't work, so I thought to try what I did with Toothless. Maybe if I spoke less, they would let me go. I prayed for Toothless to come back. He was the only one who knew where I was.

Two others joined the one in front of me who was still whispering prayers to his god. They started talking, but I couldn't make out what they were saying. One had a small white cup in his hand. Maybe there was some truth to what Clint had told me. Devil worshippers. The one with the cup moved toward me. I didn't want to drink cat's blood. I shut my eyes, clamped down hard on my lips. The rim of the cup was cold against my mouth, trying to break through. The harder I pushed my lips together, the harder the cup was forced between them.

The cup broke through, the cold metal chipping my teeth. The liquid was bitter. *Is this what cat's blood tastes like?* My stomach turned and forced its contents back out. I opened my eyes and found two eyes staring back at me. The one holding the cup stood behind the one in front of me, who shouted to give me more because I wasn't keeping the bitter stuff down. The cup holder gave me a backhand across my face and pinched my nose. When I had to open my mouth for air he threw the rest of the bitter drink down my throat.

Again, I tried telling them I had done nothing wrong, but they shoved balled-up socks into my mouth and secured them with tape around my head.

It didn't take long for me to drift off.

The singing and chanting woke me. The hooded figures were circled around the fire, feet stomping, hands clapping and beating against their Bibles. For a moment I forgot I was tied up and tried to stand, but I couldn't. They've fed me that liquid for the past three days.

"Wake up! You're dreaming," I told myself.

8

BUSINESS WITH RICHARD

Tuesday

On Tuesday afternoon Gershwin walked up the driveway at number 3 Dyster Street. He passed the gardener on his knees, pulling out weeds. Gershwin said "Hello, mister," but the man ignored his greeting and continued his work. He reached the front door and put his ear against it, listening for any signs of life before he knocked. Gershwin was nervous. The church was their usual meeting spot. He was comfortable meeting his clients in their cars, in alleyways, and in the shadows. He was shocked that Pastor Richard had asked that he come to his house.

"Pastor Richard? It's me, Gershwin," he said, knocking on the front door. He looked through the keyhole.

His shoulders slumped when he heard clicking heels approaching. Gershwin pulled the blue thumb drive out of his back pocket, armed and ready for the fight coming to him. The door flung open.

"Good afternoon, Mrs. Stroebel," he said. He tried to smile, but it died off slowly to mirror the stern face of the woman standing in front of him.

"What do you want?" demanded the pastor's wife, Pearl. "We don't want your kind here."

"What kind is that?" asked Gershwin. Without waiting for her answer, he gave her the thumb drive and said, "I brought this for Pastor Richard." His forehead pulled down in a frown as his eyes ran up and down over the woman. *Since when does a pastor's wife look like this?* His eyes followed the line her bra made under her see-through white blouse.

Under Gershwin's stare, Pearl smoothed out invisible creases in her blouse. She grabbed for the thumb drive, but Gershwin held on to it a little bit longer than necessary and forced a smile to his lips. "I think it's best I give it to him myself," he said.

"Sorry, but he's busy," said Pearl. "I don't have time for this! So whatever you need to give him you can give to me."

"But he instructed me to bring it to him directly."

"Well, you can give it to me or not at all. I have better things to do than stand here and wait around for you to decide what you're gonna do," said Pearl, and again she tried to grab the thumb drive out of his grip. When she was unsuccessful she took a step back and closed the front door.

Gershwin's jaw dropped in shock. He turned around and started to walk away, but as he descended the stairs down from the porch the front door swung open again.

"Gershwin, so sorry," said Pastor Richard. "Please excuse my wife. She's been like this the entire week. She thinks the gardener stole her cellphone, and she refused to accept my offer to buy her a new one," he explained. "Everything was fine this morning. She had stopped sulking, but now I don't know what's happening. Come inside." He stepped aside to let Gershwin in.

"Richard, I'm off," said Pearl, appearing behind her husband. "I'll call you when I get to my sister's."

Gershwin smirked when he saw the fear bubbling up in Pastor Richard's eyes. It reminded him of a child who'd gotten caught doing something they weren't supposed to. He faked a cough to hide the laughter pushing up his throat.

"I'm sorry, please give me a minute. She was supposed to leave early this morning, but ..." Pastor Richard turned to pick up Pearl's suitcase, which was standing next to the beige couch.

"No, leave it!" Gershwin heard Pearl say through the door Pastor Richard had left ajar. "I can do it myself. Just keep that *thing* out of my house."

Pastor Richard watched his wife grab her car keys from the dining table, rush down the corridor, and disappear into the kitchen. He heard the kitchen door to the garage open and close, and waited until he heard the car's engine before he opened the front door. By now Gershwin was sitting cross-legged on the porch, his attention on the gardener pulling weeds.

"Come inside," Pastor Richard said. Gershwin stood up and entered the house.

"Piet, that will be all for today," Pastor Richard told the old man crouched over, tending to his wife's garden. He walked down the steps and pushed a fifty-rand note into the man's hand. "This is for today. The madam will return next Monday, so come by then, okay?" Excited to attend to his guest waiting inside, Pastor Richard hurried back up the steps as the old man picked up a garbage bag filled with grass cuttings.

Finally, alone, Gershwin thought, as he watched from the front entry.

"Get inside," said Pastor Richard. "You know the Shadows have eyes everywhere." He closed and locked the door behind him and walked down the corridor. "Let's go to my study," he told Gershwin, who was inspecting the three-seater beige couch taking up centre stage in the living room. Gershwin's gaze followed Richard's silhouette in the flat-screen TV hanging on the wall.

"She really loves her beige," said Gershwin. He dropped his backpack at the entrance and followed Richard's retreating footsteps while he inspected the smiling couple dressed in wedding attire in the framed photos running down the corridor wall.

"She looks happy," he said to himself. He stopped for a

few seconds in front of the centrepiece portrait and pushed one of its corners to straighten it out, but it tilted again. He left the portrait as he found it, angled slightly to one side.

"So you're gonna keep me waiting?" asked Pastor Richard.

"What really happened between the two of you?" asked Gershwin, strolling into the study. "And I don't want the story you gave me last time."

"I don't want to talk about my wife," said Pastor Richard. "Let's leave that for another day."

Gershwin dropped onto the love seat next to the window. He kicked his shoes off and threw one leg after the other over the armrest.

"You see how she is," said Pastor Richard, pulling his shirt free from his pants. "She changed after we lost Riana." Gershwin followed Pastor Richard's eyes to a portrait of a laughing toddler dressed in a white suit hanging on the wall.

"This was her room. It would've been her fifth birthday this year," said Pastor Richard. "The last time Pearl was in here was the night before Riana drowned." He grew quiet and closed the study door. He walked over to Gershwin, who was still looking at the portrait.

"I thought you said you didn't want to talk about it?" Gershwin said.

"Sometimes it's good to talk to someone who really wants to listen," Pastor Richard said, and pushed Gershwin's legs off the armrest. He spread Gershwin's legs and knelt in front of him.

"Pastor Stroebel," said Gershwin, "don't you think it would be better if we just talked this time? It seems like you have a lot on your mind, and I'm right here ready to listen to your every word." Gershwin played with the grey curls on the pastor's head.

"No, don't worry about me. I'm fine," he said. "But if you're gonna keep me waiting like this, then that might change." Gershwin threw his arms around the man kneeling in front of him. "Maybe you can help me to feel even better," Pastor Richard said, and pushed his moist lips against Gershwin's. The pastor stood up, took Gershwin's hand, and pulled him up. He walked Gershwin to his desk. Gershwin closed the Bible and moved it and some papers to one side before he sat down on the desk.

He threw his legs around Pastor Richard's waist. "Is this what you need?" Gershwin said, and kissed down the side of his neck. He smelled brandy and coffee on Pastor Richard breath. "Have any more of that brandy?"

Pastor Richard took hold of Gershwin's hands and kissed them, before making his way around the desk. He pulled out the brown leather chair, sat down, and opened the bottom drawer. He took out a half-full bottle of brandy, filled two glasses from the water tray standing on a small table behind the desk, and placed the brandy back in the drawer. Before he closed the drawer, the pastor noticed Pearl's cellphone at the back and pushed a file over it. He hadn't gotten around to getting the video off his wife's phone, and then putting it somewhere she would find it again. But now with her away he'd be able to remove the video clip and replace her cellphone and stop her complaining.

"Hello!" said Gershwin. "Are you still with me?"

Pastor Richard closed the drawer and pushed one of the glasses into Gershwin's hand. He relaxed back in the chair and sipped the brandy, then put the glass on the desk and unzipped his pants. Gershwin pulled the thumb drive out of his jeans pocket and threw it on the Bible.

"Maybe you should stop playing games and give me what I pay for," said Pastor Richard.

"What are you preaching this week?" asked Gershwin, unbuttoning his jeans. Pastor Richard smiled as Gershwin's package popped out and he pulled his pants down to his ankles. "Are you preaching about Sodom and Gomorrah?" Gershwin laughed, lowering himself onto Richard's lap.

"Maybe you should come over and say a prayer with me," answered Pastor Richard.

They froze at the sound of a knock on the front door.

"Are you expecting anyone?" Gershwin asked.

"Shhh…" Pastor Richard stared at his study door. He lifted Gershwin off and pushed him onto the desk, zipped up his pants, and grabbed his shirt.

Another knock, this time louder and more impatient.

"Don't move!" said Pastor Richard. "Probably the gardener. And put on your clothes," he hissed as he slipped out of the study, closing the door behind him.

But didn't he leave? Gershwin wondered. He wriggled

slowly off the desk, accidentally dragging one of the glasses with him.

"Shit!" he exclaimed. He pulled on his clothes as he searched for something to clean up the spilled liquor.

He opened the desk drawer and scratched around inside. "Oh god! Where's the tissues?"

Gershwin saw a piece of rolled-up toilet paper underneath the brandy bottle to catch any drips. He looked nervously at the door to make sure it was still closed. He didn't want to further anger Pastor Richard. *Why did he act like that anyway?* The pastor had never pushed Gershwin away before. Gershwin was grateful for the thick carpet that had saved the glass from breaking. He cleaned the spill and threw the soggy toilet paper in the bin standing against the wall behind the desk. He knew Pastor Richard would smell the spilled liquor when he came back. Gershwin sat down in the chair and drank from the glass that still had brandy in it. He pulled out the bottle and filled the glasses again. Gershwin tightened the bottle's cap and pushed it back into the drawer, but it wouldn't fit like before. He opened the drawer a little wider and saw a file lying awkwardly. He straightened the file, and then he saw it. A beige cellphone tucked away at the back of the drawer. *Why didn't he give her this cellphone to use?* Gershwin thought. *It would suit her nicely with the rest of the beige*, he joked to himself.

"Maybe it's broken," he said out loud, just as the cellphone started vibrating. "What the hell?" Gershwin picked up the phone. Fear roared in his ears, warning him that Pastor Richard would be back any minute. He opened the study door slightly and listened for any movement coming from the front of the house. Grumbling whispers, that was all he heard. He closed the door as quietly as he could and hurried back to the chair. An urge inside him fought against his fear of Pastor Richard walking in on him doing something he wasn't supposed to. The urge won. He tapped on the side of the cellphone and the screen came alive. Relief washed over Gershwin when he saw that the cellphone didn't ask for any authentication.

His face creased in confusion when he noticed the wallpaper on the cellphone. Is this Pearl's cellphone? But why does he have it? And why is it hidden in his drawer? he asked himself. *The only one with the answers might not like the fact that you know about the cellphone in the first place*, his fear answered back. It didn't make sense, so his thumb continued furiously navigating around the screen. The low-battery alert vibrated. No, not now, Gershwin thought.

He read a message that was addressed to Pearl. A smile crept onto his face as he scrolled through the gallery. Gershwin tapped on the only video saved to the cellphone. He turned up the volume. Singing and praying crawled through the speaker. *Not another Jesus party.* Gershwin sighed inwardly. The video zoomed in on a fire in the background. He squinted at the screen, trying to understand what he was seeing.

"The fuck?" he muttered.

The low-battery alert warned him again and stopped the video from playing further. Gershwin's thumbs flew over the screen as a new curiosity woke inside him. He tapped on the caller app to check if the cellphone had any airtime. He needed to send the video to himself. His fingers tapped furiously on the screen. He remembered that Pastor Richard had recently had Wi-Fi installed. He tapped the screen and Pearl's phone connected without any issues.

Gershwin heard Pastor Richard's voice rising in volume but couldn't make out what was being said. *I'll send the video through WhatsApp*, he thought. His fingers flowed from one screen to the next, excited to send the video to himself, only to realize that he didn't remember his own number. The only number he knew by heart was Sara's. He had saved her number under his own name and he laughed at the idea of Pearl finding his name on her cellphone. Gershwin first pressed the share button and then send.

Completely absorbed, Gershwin didn't hear the pastor come down the corridor, open the door, and enter the room.

"What the fuck are you doing?" he asked, seeing his wife's cellphone in Gershwin's hands.

"Nothing," Gershwin said, lowering his hands into his lap. "I'm waiting for you."

"What's in your hands?" asked Pastor Richard, anger darkening his face.

"Why do you have your wife's cellphone?" Gershwin asked. "Didn't you say that it was stolen? And that she's angry about it?" He got up and walked to the other side of the desk where Pastor Richard was frozen in place. He tried caressing the pastor's face. "Was it to get her away from here so we could be alone?"

"What gives you the right to look in places not meant for your eyes?" Pastor Richard demanded, grabbing Gershwin's arm. "I invite you into my home and you invade my privacy?"

"Richard, you're hurting me," said Gershwin, trying to break free from the pastor's grip.

"What are you doing with that cellphone?" Pastor Richard snatched the phone out of Gershwin's hand and pushed him. Gershwin stumbled backward.

"If this is the way you're gonna treat me, then I think it's best I leave," said Gershwin. "You don't need to act like this. No one knows I'm here. Maybe—"

"Maybe what?" asked Pastor Richard.

Gershwin's discomfort kept him quiet.

"I'm gonna ask you for the last time," Pastor Richard warned, and tapped on the cellphone's screen. "What are you doing with this cellphone?"

Gershwin started moving toward the door. "You don't have to pay me," he said, regretting he hadn't deleted the WhatsApp message after sending it.

"I asked you a question!" screamed Pastor Richard. "Where do you think you're going?"

"Richard, I didn't do anything. I was looking for tissues

and saw the cellphone and it vibrated and I'd only started checking it when you came in," lied Gershwin, shuffling discreetly toward the door. He knew he had seen something that he wasn't supposed to see and he needed to get out. "I think I'm gonna go," said Gershwin, checking the distance between himself, the door, and the pastor. *I'll make it*, he thought, as shivers ran down his spine, screaming at him to get out. He made a break for the study door, but Richard was closer and kicked the door shut.

"Richard!" cried Gershwin. "I said I want to leave."

"And I asked you what you were doing with the cellphone." Pastor Richard's face was masked in anger. He approached Gershwin, who was stepping backward, still hoping to find an exit. *The window*, Gershwin thought, and turned to see black bars to deter burglars staring back at him. *Where did those come from?* he thought. *They weren't there earlier.*

Pastor Richard grabbed Gershwin from behind and swung him around. "I asked you what you did with the cellphone," he said, landing a punch on Gerswhin's face.

Gershwin fought back, but his blows did nothing to Pastor Richard, who was sturdier than him. Pastor Richard handed out the punches and Gershwin defended by ducking and diving. They ended up on the carpet, but not in the way Gershwin had imagined they would. Pastor Richard pinned Gershwin to the floor.

Gershwin fought against him. "Richard, please ... Richard, I can't ..." he choked, forcing the words through the grip tightening around his throat. Gershwin kicked his legs, but the pastor's weight grew heavier and heavier with every second that went by.

"Stay out of other people's business," Pastor Richard said to Gershwin's silenced body.

9

THE VIDEO

Tuesday

Nique was relaxing on Sara's bed with her back against the wall. She looked up from her cellphone as Sara's mother peeked her head into the room.

"When are you free, Aunty Jen, so I can do your hair?" asked Nique, trying not to focus on Jen's paisley headscarf.

"Oh, Nique, if only I had the time to look all fancy. I'll leave that to you youngsters. I had my time," she said, awkwardly pushing bits of her hair back under her headscarf. "And besides, I can't cook with my hair all over the place. Imagine if someone found a hair in one of their samosas! Ooh, no. I couldn't." Jen disappeared down the corridor into the kitchen.

Sara's cellphone beeped. She picked it up and swiped over the screen.

"Ooh, who's looking for you?" Nique teased. "Is it Rosco again?"

Sara just continued tapping her phone's screen.

"Why do you look so confused?" Nique prodded.

"I'm not sure. Someone sent me a video clip on WhatsApp," said Sara. "It says it's from Gershwin, but this isn't Gershwin's number. Do you know this number?" Sara handed the phone to Nique.

"Hm, I don't recognize it," said Nique.

"Why would Gershwin send me a message from a different number?" asked Sara, taking the phone back. "What the hell? Where's the sound?"

"Turn up the volume!" Nique said, and took the phone out of Sara's hand and pressed the side. The sound of chanting and prayers crept out of the speaker.

"I know how to work my cellphone, thank you very much," Sara said, and took her phone back, curious to see what she was hearing.

"I know, I know. But can you make out what's going on there?" said Nique. "Just be careful, it might be a virus."

"A virus?" scoffed Sara. "Who would send me a virus. It's probably just one of those chain-letter jokes going around on WhatsApp. You know, the one where nothing happens, then suddenly a monster appears on your screen?"

"LOL," said Nique. "Then it must be from Rosco."

"Who's Rosco?" Jen asked stepping into Sara's room.

"This is the second time I've heard you mention a Rosco."

Nique and Sara looked at each other.

"Hi, Aunty Jen. He's just a guy who lives down the street," said Nique.

"Do I know his mother? And why is he calling you, Sara?" Jen's eyes jumped between her daughter and Nique.

"Yes, Aunty Jen, you must know his family. They have the corner shop on Hope Street," Nique said.

"Oh, okay," Jen said, and went back to the kitchen.

"Nique!" Sara exclaimed.

"What? That's where they live," said Nique.

"Yeah, but you know I don't want her to know my business." Sara threw the phone onto her desk.

"Wait, don't you want to see what the clip is about?" Nique picked up the phone and relaxed back onto the bed. "What the fuck is going on here?"

"Just lower the volume, please," said Sara.

"Sara!" cried Nique. "Look at this." She stood up to show Sara the screen. The two friends stood in silence as they watched the video clip. "Girl, hand me your earbuds," instructed Nique. "I want to hear what they're saying." Nique put on the earbuds and gasped a moment later. "What the hell is going on here? Who sent you this thing?"

"You're asking me?" said Sara. "They look like devil worshippers."

"What's wrong?" Jen asked, as she re-entered the room after hearing the commotion. Drying her hands with a dish towel, she hung over Sara's shoulder to see what

122

they were watching. "Where's the sound? I can't hear anything."

Nique pulled out the earbuds, and the praying and singing mixed with screams blared through the speaker.

"Did you hear that?" cried Sara.

"What now?" said Jen.

"Mom, it sounded like someone was calling my name."

"Why would they call your name? No, it's just your imagination," said Nique. "What's wrong with these people? Do they have pillowcases over their heads?"

"Oh, my god! Is that a person tied to a tree?" asked Jen.

All three women gasped at the same time when the tree and the person tied to the trunk caught fire.

"Is this real?" asked Sara as the painful shrieks of the person on fire were drowned out by the singing and chanting growing louder. "It must be a movie," she said. "People wouldn't do something like this in real life, right?" Her eyes focused on Nique, who was standing with her hand over her mouth.

"I don't know, Sara, but it doesn't look like that was fake," said Nique. "Aunty Jen, do you know this number?" She showed her the WhatsApp number the video had been sent from. "It said the message was from Gershwin, but this isn't our Gershwin's number. He would've told us if he had a new number."

"Wait, that number looks familiar. I'll get my cell-phone and check my contacts."

"Could that be the body they found on the rugby field yesterday morning?" asked Nique.

"Have you tried calling the number?" asked Jen, coming back into Sara's bedroom.

"No, not yet," said Sara. "No minutes. We'll need to send this video to Ley."

"Give me the number so I can try calling it," said Jen. Nique read out the number, and Jen pushed the green call button on her cellphone. "Pearl? That can't be right."

"You have this number saved in your contacts?" asked Sara.

"Did you give me the right number?" asked Jen. "Please read it again." Sara took her mother's phone and compared the two numbers.

"How would Pearl know my number?" asked Sara, handing her cellphone to Nique. "And why would she send me something like this?"

Jen tapped on her screen again and lifted the cellphone to her ear.

"Voice mail," she said. "Maybe her phone was stolen?"

"We need to call Ley," said Nique. "She'll know what to do."

Jen took her phone back from Sara and left to tend to her samosas.

"Do you think it could be Carl?" Nique asked, breaking the silence they were sitting in.

"No!" cried Sara. "Don't think like that."

"Where's Gershwin?" asked Nique, looking at the unread WhatsApp messages she had sent him earlier that day.

"He's probably at home," answered Sara. "I know what you're thinking, but that can't be Carl."

"Sara, we don't know that," replied Nique. "It could be anyone. Wait, I need to go. The twin sisters down Main Road booked me for a wash and blow." Nique grabbed her bag and went to the kitchen to say goodbye to Jen. She left the house trying to squish a foil-wrapped parcel into her bag.

"I can always count on Aunty Jen to have snacks," Nique said to Sara, who was leaning her arms on the fence outside.

"You know her. Why do you think Aunty Merle is here every day." Sara laughed. She lit a cigarette and blew out circles of blue smoke. Nique tossed her bag on the cement wall and joined her friend in staring out into the street.

"Don't you have to be somewhere?" Sara asked.

"It's not like I have to take a taxi or catch a train to get there," said Nique. "And you know them, always late. Besides, I can't get that scream out of my head."

They fell silent as they stared out into the street alive with people. Children dressed in school uniforms rushed home after school. A group of older women congregated on the other side of the street, whispering together, all dressed in different coloured checkered kitchen aprons, headscarves covering their hair. They broke out into laughter, and then their voices lowered to whispers again. A group of teenage boys strolled by, acting wiser than they were. Another group of teenage boys stood at the corner shop next door, some sharing a cigarette and the others begging for money. A gangster-turned-pastor dressed in a suit that was too small for him and a bright red tie was reading out of a Bible lying open in one of his hands. "Jesus will show you the way," the two women heard him advise the boys.

People who'd lost the fight against meth floated like autumn leaves down the street, no one paying them any mind.

Nique and Sara watched the sun set behind the colourful three-storey apartment block standing in front of Table Mountain.

"And you say there's nothing beautiful here," Sara said.

10

IN THE SHADOWS

Last Sunday

I think I've been here for almost a week The sun comes up, and then it dips again. Most of the time, two of them watch over me. The piece of tarp they threw over me kept most of the cold out at night. The only fuck-up is the pissing. They don't bother to clean me. I've grown used to the smell of the piss and the shit. What else could I do? I don't know if the cold shivers I'm feeling are because I'm sitting in my own piss, or because of the fear of being tied to a tree and covered with a tarp, or because the dragon is dying inside of me. The balled-up socks they forced into my mouth have soaked up all my spit. I have no feeling in my jaw. They give me water at least, so I should be grateful. And they've given me a few pieces of bread. Just enough so I don't die of hunger. But I read somewhere that you can go without food for a long time before you'd die of starvation. So they're keeping me alive by bringing water. I cried, begged, promised I'd do anything they want, but it didn't help. So I gave up pleading, promising, and crying. Now I'm just waiting for what's next. It can't be worse than this. The bitter stuff they gave me to drink wasn't cat's blood. It was clear, like water. The singing and the praying only start at night. And that's when they force the bitter stuff down my throat. I wish death would come because what are they waiting for? It would just be easier if I were dead.

I guess Death is standing next to you when you can think of nothing else. The TV says that when you die, your life flashes before your eyes. I never thought I'd experience that. I'm still too young. I don't want to die. God, if you're there, please help me. I hear the hooded ones praying, but I'm not sure if they're praying to the same god I am. What moments from your life flash before your eyes when you go?

I remember when the apartments were brand new, shining with colour and the promise of a better future. I always wondered why they plastered a name like the Shadows on the place we had to call home. Maybe it was the white people's way of reminding us of our place in their country. Maybe they felt that it was their job to keep us in the dark so we wouldn't have the will to shine our own light. Maybe it was their way of mocking us by showing us that we'd always just be in their shadows.

We called them Fatty's Block. How do you forget someone like Fatty? They found him dead on the field after his father took his life. The field eventually became the place where they built the apartments. Life dealt him the worst hand. His dad was the one who abused him and eventually killed him. There were those who feared living there and who warned and joked that Fatty's ghost would haunt the place. But still, most of the people wanted to live there. They could not stop talking about how much better everything would be in the Shadows.

Mom was one of the people who wanted to live there. She dreamed about it and sent in her application to get an apartment. On the third floor, looking out over the Shadows, with a view as far as the bay area. But it wasn't like we didn't have a charming home already. I think Mom was caught in a dream of living higher than all her problems.

Mom, she was the best. Time and again, I would find her in the kitchen, dancing to the beat of a song only she could hear. Her dance partner, a dish towel. She always tried to get me to dance with her. She would grab my hand and swing me in circles around the kitchen table. My feet could never keep up and always lost their way halfway through. She gave the best hugs. She would hold me tight and tell me how much she loved me. I felt safe there, in her arms. But I always pulled away, out of her embrace, because boys shouldn't be cuddled by their mother. I would then hang over the bottom half of the kitchen door, watching her. She would grab that old dish towel again, one corner in each hand. It was always the same one. The red-and-white-checkered dish towel. I always told Mandy to listen to the way Mom would talk to the dish towel, but Mandy would just roll her eyes and chase me away, telling me to go and play.

Dad died when I started high school. He was the quiet one, subdued under his own issues, until he had a couple bottles of beer: only then would his words flow. Mom always scolded Mandy because she was like Dad—quiet. Even now, with all her drinking, she's still the quiet one, at home with her latest boyfriend, drinking up every cent they get. Mom always told her to dream because dreams give you a reason to smile. I can still hear her voice: "You have to have dreams, my child." And when Mandy rolled her eyes at Mom, she would turn to me and say, "I know you'll always have dreams, my baby boy."

The bitter liquid they make me drink tastes stronger tonight. The voices singing at the fire seem louder, happier. Maybe the day is coming when they'll set me free.

Another day goes by with the sun rising and dipping and rising again. It feels like I've been here longer than a week. I tried to keep count, but I lost track. The days and nights all feel the same. They came to give me water again. They threw the piece of tarp they covered me with to one side. I told one of the men I needed to piss, but as usual he laughed and told me that I'm free to do my thing because I'm not going anywhere anytime soon.

I wonder if Death ever needs to piss. People think Death is a man, but I doubt it. My mother was the one who always showed me the way, even after Death took her. Mothers always lead the way. That's why I know Death is a woman. I wish I could have met Death when she was still human. I wonder what stories she'd tell about her life. Maybe she liked tea more than coffee. Maybe she never wanted kids. Imagine if Death had a dog named Snowy with a fuzzy white coat, big brown eyes, and a pink bow on her head?

I wonder what Death looks like without her cloak on. You only ever see Death dressed up in the black cloak and holding a scythe. Almost like Death isn't Death, but the cloak and the scythe she carries. That's what the TV teaches. It's not people killing people, but the guns that kill people. It's like meth. Everyone blames me and not the drug. They only see Carl and not what meth is doing to Carl.

I wish the shivers would stop. I wish the cold would climb out of my skin. How can these people be so heartless?

I wonder if they think of Death. I wonder if they smell her the way I do. And, no, Death doesn't smell like rotting flesh, but like the sweet aromas of my childhood home. A cake baking in the oven while Mom dances in the kitchen. The gentle whiff of Dad's cigarette smoke hanging in the air. The early morning salty mist drifting in from the coast. The firewood crackling in the braai. Death smells like my first kiss, which took place just outside the kitchen door: warm breath, mint chewing gum, and sweaty palms.

I wonder if Mandy remembers the day we got lost at the beach. It was New Year's Eve, and Dad was drunk. His drinking got worse as he got older. His year always ended the same way. The paint factory he worked at would close for the holidays. He would get his bonus, bring it home, and use the rest of his pay for alcohol to get him through the break. It was kind of like he was making up for the days he couldn't drink during the year. Nothing else mattered during that time. He would get up, drink, sleep, wake up with a hangover, and drink again, restarting the cycle. After a while, Mom couldn't take it anymore and kicked him out. His jokes always turned into something else with Mom. She tried to hide the blue marks under thick makeup, but I saw the sadness in her eyes. He never hurt her in front of us. Sometimes it felt like she believed that she had to keep quiet to be a good, obedient wife to her husband.

It's funny how we try to hide the bad and shameful things that happen to us in our lives. The bruises and sores that become life lessons. It's funny how we hold on to those memories. All of them coming back now is probably Death's way of letting me know that she's here with me.

It was the same thing every year. The excitement would build leading up to Christmas, when everyone got one gift. Then we spent Boxing Day with friends and family, and the next week everyone and their grandma went to the beach for New Year's Eve. We would get up in the early morning hours because there were only a few good spots next to the barbecue stands. But getting up early was a small price to pay to spend a day at the beach, free to eat chips and sweets for the entire day, sometimes even an ice cream cone.

Every New Year's our family went to the beach with my mother's sister. Mom always said that we must be nice to our cousins and Aunty Sanna because she did a lot for us, but I never could see what she did, other than acting like her kids were better than us. And that day nothing was different. As usual, Dad made sure his case of beers was safe and secure under the makeshift gazebo we made with a red-checkered blanket, and Mom started the fire and took out the snacks. The beach was full, like it always was during the peak season. People were packed like sardines in a tin, everyone wanting to wet their feet. Almost like they needed to wash off the sins of the past year. "New year, new you," Dad like to say. But there were just too many people on that beach. If you got lost, your parents prayed that good people would find you and take you to the cops.

Aunty Sanna's kids complained about having to wait for their mother to take them swimming, and their mother always gave in to whatever her angels wanted. Aunty Sanna took Mandy and me along to swim. Afterward, she made a clear statement that her kids deserved more than us by buying ice cream only for them. She shoved the rest of her money in her bra. Mandy took my hand and squeezed it and whispered to me that she would ask Mom if we could have money for ice cream.

When we got back Mom was still flipping the meat on the fire, and Dad was still lying in the same spot where we left him, only drunker than before. It was normal for him to drink half the case of beer before lunch. Then he would take a beer-induced nap for an hour or so, and then arise fresh and ready for whatever was left over. I always wondered why grown-ups drank the way they did, until I became a grown-up the day Mom died.

Mom's cheeks grew red with embarrassment when she saw that Aunty Sanna had only treated her own kids to ice cream. I thought it would be a good time to ask Mom for money to get ice cream, but she said no. Dad heard this, staggered to his feet, and almost pushed Mom into the fire. Mom turned around to make sure that he was okay, not worried about herself, as always. Dad asked her for money to buy his kids ice cream. I didn't like the way Aunty Sanna laughed at Dad's request. It's like she knew he would act up in this way. Mom took a twenty-rand note out of her bra and handed it to him without challenging him. Dad grabbed his T-shirt that was hanging over the case of beer and threw it over his shoulders. Mom pretended that she wasn't watching his every move. He instructed us to follow him as he walked off. Mandy always looked at Mom for permission before she did anything Dad told her to do. Mom nodded her head, and Mandy took me by the hand. The farther away we walked from our spot, the tighter Mandy's grip felt.

Dad acted like he knew everyone we passed, shouting, "Happy New Year!" randomly to anyone he locked eyes with. We trailed him in silence as he walked ahead, swinging from one foot to the other. He didn't once check to see if we were behind him. And he didn't see the piece of wood that came out of nowhere. A bare-chested man with a low-hanging belly, thick arms, and no sign of a neck shouted at Dad, demanding to know why Dad had smacked his wife's ass. Dad just laughed and sang, "Happy New Year!" and turned to walk away. The piece of wood landed square between his head and shoulders.

The fat man picked up his piece of wood, whispered a few words to Dad, and left. People started gathering around Dad, and the more people gathered, the farther away we were pushed from him. Mandy started crying and told me that we must go and fetch Mom. As Dad lay bleeding on the ground, I begged Mandy through my tears for us to stay with him because it was my fault for wanting ice cream. If I hadn't put Dad on the spot to defend his poverty, he would still be drinking beer and making bad jokes. But Mandy didn't want to listen and told me again that we must go fetch Mom. I remember the fear on Mandy's face, which was so much like Dad's, her big nose, wide mouth, and dimples in her cheeks that never disappeared, even when she was angry. But she had inherited from Mom the shape and colour of her eyes. Eyes that could never hide what she was feeling. Always looking at the world with insecurity mixed with hope. Always searching for the next person to help.

I told Mandy that I needed to go to the toilet, but her need to get Mom was greater than mine, so she never really heard what I was saying, only telling me, "Just hold it, we'll go now."

Have you ever felt the world slow down and stop, as though you're trapped in a moment?

Dad was lying in his own blood in a place where no one else knew his name. Where he was just another drunk with a bleeding head. Mandy was swivelling left and right, trying to find Mom's red-checkered blanket, and I was standing anchored to one spot as my legs and feet were bathed in the warm piss streaming down. Humiliation will always be humiliation, and a pissy pants will always be a pissy pants. And a meth head will always be a meth head. Nothing can save me now, not even the Bible and its promises.

Maybe Death is one of them, Bible in hand, pillowcase covering her skull, waiting for the lamb to be slaughtered. The hooded ones placed containers next to me. I can smell the petrol. The men were laughing and chatting as they made and tended the fire. I never thought this would be the way I would meet Death. I always thought if I stuck with meth, my life would get better—just like the way I felt the first time I used. Maybe the scythe was Death's birthright. Maybe meth was mine. Maybe this was the only way for my road to end.

It was like Death walked with me the whole way here. That's probably why Toothless didn't speak to me much— because he knew where he was leading me. He felt Death around us and knew what was waiting for me. Toothless always told me Clint would lead me to my death. But what did I care about dying when Clint was always there, ready with my next hit? Clint assured me that if I looked after him, he'd be there for me. I often wondered why Clint had the power to walk through a rain of bullets and come out on the other side without a scrape on him. He always won any fight he took on. Maybe he knew Death on a personal level. He always showed off the tattoo of Death on his forearm. I think if I wasn't hooked on meth, I would've seen Clint's true colours a long time ago. I would've noticed just how fucked-up he is in the head. But Toothless was the one who led me to my death in the end.

Who would've thought there were people like this living in the Shadows? What will Sara think? She always wants to see the best in people. There's always a reason for people's behaviour, but what reason did I give them to do this to me? What reason do they have to do this, pillowcases hiding their faces, Bibles in hand? Did they forget about our god that sees what they're doing?

Maybe Death is the god everyone is so scared of. I wish I knew Death when she had a name. I wish I knew Death when she could feel. I wish she could speak to me right now. Maybe if I knew her back then, she would help me get out of this.

How do you breathe when your body is burning?

11

THE NOTE

Thursday

A lot had changed since Nique and Sara last saw each other. It had been a couple of days since Sara received the video of the person being burned to death. Gershwin had kept them at a distance, ignoring them on WhatsApp. And Carl was still missing. Nique and Sara were standing in Sara's front yard, resting with their arms on the cement fence. Nique's big white bag was lying on the ground between the two friends. Both had a cigarette burning between their fingers, floating in and out of their mouths for a drag every ten to thirty seconds. Their eyes were swollen and red from crying. Sara had thought the note was a joke when she first read it. Her mom had found it earlier that morning in their mailbox.

It was addressed to Sara and Nique, their names in big bold letters on the envelope.

Sara took the note out of her pocket and read it to herself again.

Dear Sara and Nique,

If you're reading this, then it means I had the guts to do it. I can't live like this anymore. I love you.

Gershwin

P.S. Don't worry. This is for the best.

"I don't understand what he thought..." said Sara. She pushed a wad of tear-soaked tissues into her jeans pocket. She pulled the pack of cigarettes closer and started tapping it on the palm of her hand. "Nique, why did he do it? You said he was fine."

"Girl, if we hold on to 'if onlys' and 'whys' about Gershwin, then we're gonna join him in his grave," said Nique. "You know, I made a friend while I was in Joburg. Her name was Josey. She finally took her life after struggling with addiction. Josey taught me that nothing outside of yourself can save you if you don't wanna be saved. There is nothing the people who love you can do to change that. And sometimes knowing that it's all up to you makes it harder to continue living. You know what she told me two weeks before she died from a drug overdose? Josey said, 'The next hit I take is gonna kill me,' and it did."

"But Nique, Gershwin wasn't on drugs," said Sara. "I'm sorry about your friend, but Gershwin had dreams and plans to get out of the Shadows and make a life for himself."

"I know."

"We could've done something for Gershwin," said Sara. "I mean, if only he'd talked to us. I mean … This note doesn't even sound like the Gershwin we knew."

"Sara, I know you're hurting, but there's nothing we could've done. That's what I'm trying to say," said Nique. "People can look like they're handling things in life. They can laugh and go on like things are good, but the struggle inside is real. The last time I saw Josey, she was fine. I went with her to her NA meeting. That day she was good, but her addiction had other plans for her. It's like she was no longer there, she was just a shell of her struggles walking around, biding time, waiting for that last hit. I guess the only time she was free from the pain and the hurt was when she took a hit. That's why I understand what Carl's going through."

"I'm telling you, something doesn't feel right about this."

"Yeah, you're right. Something doesn't feel right. I mean, Gershwin was ready to move. Most of his things were packed. He was ready to move out of his mother's house on Sunday. " Nique grew quiet and flicked her dead butt into the street. She grabbed a cigarette from the pack lying on top of her bag and struck the lighter's wheel a few times before the flint sparked and a small flame popped up. She drew hard on the cigarette, inhaled, and blew the smoke out her nose while filling her lungs again with another puff.

"I guess you could say he's still moving out, just maybe not the way we thought he would." Nique's eyes followed a group of boys, laughing and cracking jokes with each other. *Time stands still for nothing*, Nique thought.

"Hello, ladies," one of them called out.

Neither Nique nor Sara acknowledged the greeting.

"So you're not gonna say hello to the love of your life?" Nique teased.

"Nique, he's not the love of my life," said Sara. "I don't know…"

"What don't you know? You already hooked up with Rosco, didn't you?"

"Who said so?"

"Who do you think? Gersh—" Nique's smile died on her face as she looked down the street. "He was still okay then. He didn't say it, but he was excited to see Pastor Richard again." Nique pulled a pack of tissues out of her bag, placed the lit cigarette on the wall, and dried her tears.

"Something happened, I'm sure of it. He was so determined to get out of his mother's house. Something happened…" Sara repeated.

"She's telling everyone he hanged himself, but I wouldn't be surprised if she killed him. That woman… that woman, she's the devil," said Nique, wiping more tears from her eyes.

"Don't say that, Nique."

"Why not? Because she's his mother? She was never a mother to him. You know where I saw her the other night? If people knew what she was up to. If people only knew." Nique picked her cigarette up off the wall and lit it again. "Where's your lighter?"

Sara pulled a box of matches out of her pocket.

"Matches? Really? Since when?" Nique struggled to pull a match free from the small yellow-and-black cardboard box.

"Since I don't have a lighter." Sara sighed. "Don't you think we should go see if we can find anything else in his room tonight? Maybe he left something else for us."

"Even if something else did happen, do you think his mother would care? His body is still warm, and she already wants to put him in the ground. I agree. Something's not right."

"Can you believe it? The poor child. I'm sure his mother is in a state," said Merle, walking in through the front gate, her hair full of green and orange curlers. "Do you know what happened?" she asked, looking at them over the top of her glasses. Neither woman answered her. "Ley said she'll be here later tonight so we can drive with her to the wake at Gershwin's house."

"My mom is in the kitchen, Aunty Merle," said Sara.

"Yes, she asked me to come over. She called in such a panic. Almost had a heart attack," said Merle. "There's just been too much death in the Shadows over the past couple of weeks."

Sara and Nique looked at each other. "Who else died, Aunty Merle?" asked Sara.

"My word, how can you ask me that question? That friend of yours. The one who went missing. The one on drugs. What's his name again?"

"Aunty Merle, Carl is not dead," said Sara.

"My child, when a person is gone so long ... then you must know you're looking for a body," said Merle. "Hasn't he been gone for almost three weeks now?"

"But Aunty Merle, you can't just say things like that," said Nique. "It hasn't been that long. Carl will turn up," Nique said, but then she realized that it had been almost two weeks since she'd last seen Carl.

"I'm off to visit with your mother and have some of her nice roti and curry." Merle laughed and walked into the house. Nique and Sara watched her disappear behind the front door.

"I need to top up the minutes for my phone," said Sara. "The same number keeps on calling, but every time I call back there's no answer. Do you know this number? Hello, anyone home?" asked Sara, but Nique's focus was on her phone. "It's easy to tell me we need to accept what happened to Gershwin, but look at what you're doing. Reading your old conversations won't change a thing. Like you said, there was nothing we could've done. And now this nonsense about Carl."

"Who told you I was reading old conversations? Let me see the number."

"Because I know you," said Sara, handing Nique her

phone. "I'm worried about what Aunty Merle said about Carl. How can she expect us to believe that Carl is dead. Two friends in one week? Where does she get her information?"

"Girl, you know too well that Aunty Merle is the tabloid of this street," said Nique. "You can't believe anything that comes out of her mouth. Stop picking up calls from numbers you don't know," she said, and stuck a fifty-rand note in Sara's hand.

"What am I supposed to do with this?" asked Sara. "I wanna know who's calling me. It might be important."

"Suit yourself. Don't come crying to me when you get scammed. And don't think I didn't notice you're wearing lip gloss." Nique said. "Get another pack of cigarettes and get yourself a lighter, too."

"What are you talking about, Nique? Sometimes you see things that don't exist," Sara blustered. "If I want to pick up calls from numbers I don't know, or wear lip gloss to feel good about myself, it's my right," she said indignantly, and walked out the front gate.

12

THE OPEN GRAVE

Sunday

A group of people dressed in black stood in a half-circle around the back of the hearse. The ones closest to the door stood with their arms around the person standing next to them, supporting each other. Here and there eyes puffed and red looked out over dark sunglasses. The sounds of sniffles, crying, and soft whispers hung in the air. One of the three undertakers, a thin man dressed in a grey suit, opened the door of the hearse. The door seal popped as air was sucked into the hearse, and a crackle of laughter jumped out from the back of the group of mourners. Stern-looking mothers turned their heads to scold the youngsters with their eyes. "You should be ashamed of yourselves!" an older woman said, with her arms folded across her chest. The laughter turned into forced coughs.

Farther back, a group of older men stood with cupped hands as they tried to hide the smoke coming from their lit cigarettes. An undertaker pulled on the gold-plated handles decorating the brown casket, and the bottom of the casket screamed as it scraped against the metal rails on its way out of the hearse. The other undertakers joined their colleague, pushing the trolley that would transport the casket from the hearse to the grave. One of the undertakers pulled the casket onto the trolley and six people took their spots, three on each side. They simultaneously grabbed on to the handles and transported Gershwin's casket to his final resting place.

Sara turned around and walked in the opposite direction from the rest of the people following the casket. She watched the people walking down the gravel path leading to the open grave on the outer edge of the graveyard. *It would've been better if the hearse had parked closer to the grave*, she thought. She straightened the creases in the black dress she last wore at her father's funeral. The memory of her father took a seat in her mind and she searched for his gravestone. She thought of his hands that could build and fix anything. She remembered how he'd freaked out when she asked him if she could shadow him at work. "Welding isn't for girls, Sara," he'd said. She had to promise she wouldn't touch anything.

Sara pulled a pack of cigarettes and a lighter out of the bag hanging over her shoulder and followed the funeral proceedings down the gravel road. She remembered the tool shed her father had built in their backyard. Beams of sunlight would flow through the cracks and holes in the corrugated-iron roof. As a child, she had loved trying to catch the rays as they played on the dust in her dad's tool shed. Her cellphone vibrated in her bag, returning her focus to the funeral happening in front of her. She lit a cigarette and watched as the pallbearers battled with the trolley and casket on their way to the open grave.

Gershwin's mother, Rose, was giving the undertakers instructions on how to do their job. She looked like a choir leader with her arms flailing in the air, thought Sara. She thought Rose looked very calm for someone who had just lost her son. Sara watched as Ley drove in through the graveyard's gate, got out of her car, and made her way toward the gathering.

"What else do you carry around in that bag?" asked Ley as she got closer to Sara.

"Do you want one?" Sara offered, blowing out a stream of smoke.

"Weren't you supposed to be one of the pallbearers?" Ley asked, and pointed to Gershwin's casket, which was now placed on green straps hanging over the open grave.

"I just couldn't do it," said Sara. "I don't know what I did wrong, but when Rose didn't return my greeting earlier, I decided not to do it."

The two friends smoked quietly.

"Why are you so late?" Sara asked, breaking the

silence. "I didn't see you at Gershwin's house for the start of the service. Did something happen?"

"I don't know how to say this, but we now know with certainty that the body found on the rugby field is Carl's," said Ley, crushing her half-smoked cigarette beneath the sole of her black boot.

"I know, your mom told me," said Sara, tears forming in her eyes.

"Who told her? We only got the confirmation this morning," said Ley.

"You'll have to ask her."

"Have you seen Nique?" asked Ley, breaking the silence. Why isn't she here yet? The funeral is almost over and she's still not here? Didn't she sleep at your house? I need to tell her before she finds out from someone else."

"I've been sending Nique messages all day, but she only reads them and doesn't reply," said Sara, drying her tears. She showed Ley the WhatsApp messages on her cellphone.

"Come, let's go back," said Ley. "Nique knows where the graveyard is."

Sara followed Ley's zigzagging path between the graves and other mourners as they made their way to stand in the front row. She pulled a tissue out of her bag and dabbed at the tears rolling down her cheeks. She folded the wet tissue and pushed it back in her bag. Sara felt Ley's warm hand on the small of her back. Her shoulders tightened, and she shifted her body slightly away. *What will the people think?* she thought. *Ley has a fiancée and I have Rosco.* Sara touched her stomach as she thought of the future that was waiting for her. Sara felt Rose's eyes burning holes in her from where she stood next to the pastor who would lead the service.

"Pastor, can we begin?" said Rose, loud enough for everyone to hear. "We don't have the entire day to stand here."

Pastor Richard opened the Bible to Psalm 23, letting it rest in his left hand. He moved his weight from one foot to the other. He closed the Bible again. He was waiting for the three undertakers pulling and pushing the casket on the green straps to distribute the weight equally over the open grave. Pastor Richard looked up to the sky that was growing darker on the horizon, dark grey clouds floating in over Table Mountain. *That's Cape Town for you, four seasons in one day*, he thought. He looked down at the short woman standing next to him, scared she'd cause them both to fall off the small heap of black sand he had to stand on. The shape of her nose reminded him of the young man he used to see every week. The man he had to bury because of his own actions.

Rose looked up at him and Pastor Richard remembered the last time he had stared into the deep brown eyes of his lover. Maybe he would have to kill her, too. She knew too much. Rose had helped him hide his crime. He'd had to lie to her about the reason Gershwin was in his study but told her that Gershwin had sent the video to an unknown number. He'd called the number a couple of times but didn't get an answer. *I'll try again after the service, or maybe get Rose to call*, he thought. She was the one who helped him stage Gershwin's body as if he had hanged himself. She was the one who wrote the note. She told him that there was nothing to worry about because she was glad that he had done it. She was an accomplice to her son's murder. Pastor Richard hated standing next to the woman who wanted to get into his pants more than anything else. He hated the graveyard with its black sand that would end up in the weirdest places, like it soaked up all the leftover energies of the dead and had a life of its own.

He saw the woman's lips move, but his brain didn't register anything she was saying. He looked down at the black material of her dress that pulled at odd places all over her body.

"Pastor," said Rose, elbowing him in the side. "We're ready and waiting on you."

Richard flipped open the Bible. "Psalm twenty-three," he read. "The Lord is my shepherd. I shall not want..." He closed the Bible and continued reciting the psalm from memory as he watched the people standing in front of him. As he finished, he lifted the Bible in the air. The silver watch sliding slightly down his wrist caught his eye. Another memory courtesy of Gershwin. Even though he'd paid Gershwin, it was more to them than sex and money. Pastor Richard could be himself with Gershwin. *I shouldn't have done it*, he thought.

Pastor Richard stepped off the pile of sand as Rose insisted he let her speak before he gave his final words. He looked down at the sandy crust that had formed along the edges of his shiny black shoes. His eyes then jumped from person to person who stood lined up next to Gershwin's casket. No one was listening to Rose invite everyone for a cup of tea and cake after the proceedings. Some of them looked at him, whispered, and then laughed. *They know about us*, he thought. He pushed three fingers of his free hand in between his neck and his shirt collar, trying to get some air to pass into his windpipe.

Two of the undertakers moved to stand on either side of the casket. One of them looked at Richard, waiting for the go-ahead. He reminded Pastor Richard of his brother. He hadn't seen him for ten years. He wondered if he was still alive.

Pastor Richard cleared his throat. "Brothers and sisters, we are here today to lay to rest one of our own, Gershwin Theo Lawrence. He was ripped away from us by the hand of the devil. May our merciful God forgive Gershwin."

A MINIBUS TAXI STOPPED at the entrance of the graveyard. "Hey girl, when can I take you out on a date?" asked the door operator as Nique jumped out of the taxi holding a bunch of red roses with a single white rose in the centre. She was dressed in white skinny jeans, white Chucks, a white blouse, and a white fitted jacket.

"Sorry for being late, Gershwin," she said as she walked in through the graveyard's gate and down the gravel path. At the outer edge of the graveyard, she saw a group of people huddled around a purple gazebo. *Is that your final resting place?* She took a shortcut through the gravestones. A plastic flower stood in an old empty plastic bottle on a flattened piece of land, the only sign that there once was a grave there. *In life and in death we are alone, that's what it means to be human,* Nique thought.

The pastor's final words floated over Nique as she wandered between the people at Gershwin's funeral. She felt eyes on her back as she manoeuvred to the casket. Everyone, including Pastor Richard, grew quiet as they watched her every move. The undertakers were standing to the side waiting for the order to lower the casket. Nique placed the bouquet on top of the casket and pushed a white envelope between the flowers. *To Gershwin, love you always and forever,* the handwriting on the envelope read. She looked up and locked eyes with Sara. The small smile that her friend gave her motivated Nique to whisper a short prayer in honour of Gershwin. When she opened her eyes, a smile settled onto her face. "'Til we meet again, my sister," said Nique.

For the first time she looked over to the pastor and caught Rose's glare. *Not today, devil,* thought Nique. *Today you need to stay out of my way and not dare say a word to me.* Nique turned away from Gershwin's casket and started to walk to Sara and Ley. Nique didn't notice Rose hopping over to the casket. When Nique turned back, she was too late to catch the roses flying through the air.

"Who do you think you are?" Rose asked, clenched

fists hanging at her sides. "Who do you think you are putting flowers on my child's casket? I warned you not to come here. You are the reason my child is dead."

There was a synchronous gasp from the gathering. Everyone grew quiet. A light breeze lifted the black scarf off Rose's shoulder. A few people shuffled forward to get a better look at Rose standing at attention, chest heaving, next to Gershwin's casket.

"Not on my child's casket!" shouted Rose.

Nique's mouth hung open in shock. She picked up the roses and reached for the envelope that had fallen at the edge of the open grave, but before she could grasp it, a breeze scooped it into the hole in the ground. Nique threw the roses in to follow the envelope down to the bottom of Gershwin's grave.

"Sister Rose, this is not the place—" Rose didn't wait for Pastor Richard to finish his sentence and rushed around to where Nique stood to try to stop her, but she was too slow and watched in anger the triumph beaming on Nique's face.

"So what are you gonna do about it? You wanna get in and take them out?" shouted Nique. "Even in his death you want to treat Gershwin like a piece of shit."

"I told you to keep your faggot bullshit out of my house!" Rose shouted.

"What are you talking about? I'm more of a woman than you'll ever be!" screamed Nique.

"This is all because of you," said Rose. "You brought the devil into our house."

Pastor Richard tried to move closer to Rose, but he sank into the soft mound of sand and lost his balance. A group of younger people who had moved from the back to the front of the gathering to see what was going on started laughing, all standing with their cellphones out, ready to film the antics and share them. Pastor Richard fell forward against Rose, who in turn fell against Gershwin's casket. The casket moved slightly on the green straps. The undertakers, Ley, and Sara rushed over to keep the casket from moving any farther. Nique burst out laughing, imagining Gershwin standing behind his mother and cackling.

"If you wanna talk about the devil," said Nique, "then talk about the man who just pushed you." The crowd grew quiet, but some of the people snickered at Nique's outburst. "You are all so impressed by Deacon Rose, but do you know the shit she gets up to?" Nique turned to Rose and said, "Yeah, now you can't look me in the eye because you know what I'm talking about." A few men were helping Rose stand up.

"As long as I knew Gershwin, you abused him. If it wasn't for his grandma, you would've killed him a long time ago," said Nique. Ley tried to whisper in Nique's ear, but Nique waved her away, refusing to listen. "But you say that he's the pig, he's the faggot, he's the devil?" cried Nique. "Sara, why don't you tell them how Gershwin lived. Tell them how she forced him into his grave. Every day he had to hear how bad a son he was. A faggot. Sent by the devil himself. While Deacon Rose is apparently

the best and the holiest. You all come from the devil. You
and your blessed pastor." Nique glared at the man who
stepped in next to Rose.

"Ah yes, Pastor Richard. Remind us how you got to
know Gershwin at your weekly meetings," Nique said.
"Stop this Bible-thumping bullshit and tell us the truth
about what happened between the two of you."

"Nique, this is not the place. Let's respect Gerswhin's—"
Pastor Richard said, but Nique interrupted him.

"Not the place? But it was the right time and place when
you saw each other every week?" she screamed. "When
and where will be the right time and place for you?"

"Pastor?" asked Rose, her face scrunched in confusion.
"What is this *thing* talking about?"

"Deacon Rose, I don't know what *he's* talking about,"
said Richard. "And we need to finish here. I still need to
do a wedding this afternoon."

"Nique, Gershwin wouldn't want this," said Ley. "Let's
bury him. We can sort this out later."

"What? You know he would've loved this," said
Nique. "If he wasn't in that grave, he would've loved to
hear what his pastor had to say about them. He would've
wanted his mother to know the truth about him and
Pastor Richard. They're always preaching to people
about the truth after all."

"Be careful what you say next," threatened Pastor
Richard. "You have no proof of anything."

"So why are you so scared of what I'm gonna say
then?" asked Nique. "Because you know it's the truth."

"Nique!" cried Sara. "Leave it alone. What about Gersh—"

"What about Gershwin? Let me speak my mind," said Nique. "What about the reason he's even in this casket?"

"Stop talking nonsense," said Rose. She turned to Ley. "And you, you're a cop. Why can't you do something about this *thing* ruining my son's funeral? You're just standing there letting this happen! Why can't you remove this devil?"

"Deacon Rose, do you still want to say something?" asked Pastor Richard when Ley didn't reply. Rose shook her head.

"Please lower the casket," Pastor Richard instructed the undertakers. Rose and Pastor Richard started walking away.

"Look, everybody! Ask yourself what type of mother walks away from her child's grave as the casket is being lowered?" screamed Nique, tears swelling in her eyes. "I'll see you burn in hell!"

"Nique," begged Sara. "Leave it!"

Nique's threat was still hanging in the air when Sara saw two police sergeants approach Rose and Richard. One of the sergeants handcuffed Pastor Richard's wrists behind him.

"What's happening?" asked Sara. "Who called the cops?"

"But why? What are you doing?" Rose pleaded. "He's the pastor, and we still need to go do a wedding."

"Sir, we are arresting you for the murder of Carl Bosman," the sergeant said.

"The murder of Carl?" wailed Nique. She stepped forward, but Ley grabbed her arm. "Let me go, Ley."

"I asked them to wait outside the graveyard to arrest him after the funeral," said Ley. "The video you sent me—I don't know how to say this, but the victim was Carl. The number it was sent from was for the pastor's wife's cellphone. She told us her phone had been stolen and it was still gone. We searched the pastor's house and found the cellphone in his study. One of his church followers came forward and told us the entire story. I'm not supposed to tell you, so please keep it to yourselves. We'll know more when the pastor is brought before the courts."

"Why didn't you say anything earlier?" asked Sara.

"I couldn't say anything. We were still waiting on the DNA results. We needed to be sure, but now we have them. I went to inform Carl's sister first. That's why I got here so late," said Ley. "But don't worry, they'll pay for what they did!"

13

BROKEN DREAMS

A Few Months Later

"They emailed me this morning," said Sara.

"Who?" asked Nique.

"The people who want to give me the study grant," said Sara. "They want me to choose between the baby and my studies." She lowered her head to hide the tears rolling down her cheeks and played with the ring that Rosco had given her the night before. "Rosco told me he's serious about us. He wants me to keep the baby and he's willing to support me. He even started looking for a job."

"What's your mom gonna say?" asked Nique. "What about your plans, your dreams?" She picked the thick book up off the desk. "Do you think your dad would want you to give up on your dreams?"

"Nique, I know you want what's best for me, but please, let me make my own decisions," said Sara, rubbing the bump that was forming beneath her oversized T-shirt. "Studying abroad is a big opportunity, it was my way out, but what about the baby, Nique? The baby didn't ask to be here. And Rosco and I—"

The two friends stopped talking when they heard Sara's mom open the front door.

Jen popped her head into Sara's room. "Why so quiet?" she asked, setting the red-and-yellow grocery bags on the floor. She removed her big-rimmed hat, pulled an envelope from one of the bags, and handed it to Sara. "I picked this up at the post office for you," she said. Sara placed the envelope on her desk. "You're not gonna open it? It must be serious business if it came through registered mail. Aunty Fien was working at the post office, and she said that next time you'll have to come and fetch your post yourself. They're not allowed to just give your mail to anyone, even your mother."

"But you had my ID, Mommy."

"No, my child, that's the new rule."

"That's just unnecessary. What if I'm sick, or can't make it to the post office for some reason?" Sara sat down on the bed and looked at Nique for support. "Mommy, I need to talk to you."

"So, talk, I'm here," said Jen. "But why do you look so serious all of a sudden?"

Nique grabbed her bag, ready to leave.

"No, Nique. Please stay," said Sara. "I want you to be here."

"What's wrong?" asked Jen. "Didn't we go through enough bad things this year?"

Nique sat down next to Sara, took her hand, and smiled.

"Don't worry, Mommy," said Sara. "It's not bad news, or at least I don't think so."

Jen pulled the chair next to Sara's bed over to sit in front of her daughter. "Go ahead, tell me what's going on," said Jen. "You say it's not bad news, but look at your face. Please stop frowning, my child. You're too young to have stress wrinkles on your beautiful face."

"Mommy, I'm pregnant. Rosco is the father," sobbed Sara. "The people offering me the grant told me to choose between the baby or my studies. That's what the registered mail is about. I need to decide and send it back to them in a couple of days."

Jen handed Sara the tissues that were on the desk. "Sara, the only thing you can do now is what makes you happy," she said, breaking the silence in the room. "The choice is yours. You were looking for a way to get out of the Shadows, but the Shadows is in your blood, my child. It doesn't matter where you go in this world, because in the end, you'll return home. Maybe this baby is your anchor, so that you'll always remember to come home." Jen wiped the tears rolling down her daughter's cheeks with the back of her hand. "My child, you won't lose me, and I won't let you go. Everything will be okay. Don't you agree, Nique?"

"Your mother is right, Sara." Nique put her arm around

her friend's shoulders. "We've lost too much this year. We are here for you and will support you in whatever you decide to do. We're not doing it for Rosco or for the baby or for anyone else. We're here for you, Sara."

Sara stood up, opened the envelope, and pulled out the forms. "I know a lot of people will say I'm doing the wrong thing, but you are right," said Sara. "We've lost too much. I can always go back to school. I can always apply to go abroad. I can always fill in these forms again. But who knows if I'll get another chance to have a baby? I'll get another chance to go abroad." Sara took a deep breath, tore up the forms, and dumped the small heap of paper on her desk. Then she walked out of her bedroom. Jen and Nique listened to her footsteps disappearing into the bathroom and the door closing behind her.

"We've been through too much, Aunty Jen," said Nique. "Even though I wasn't at the trial, you know how people talk around here. I've heard the worst."

"Yeah, I understand, Nique," said Jen. "I heard Rose confessed after another follower came forward. Apparently, he backed up what the first witness said, and told them everything about what was going on at that church. Then Rose told on Pastor Richard, and how they planned to clean the so-called evils out of the Shadows. How can people use Jesus as an excuse to do their dirty work? Can you believe Rose hid the murder of her own child because she believed it was God's work?"

"I just want to know how she got to that point," Nique said. "She's sick to do something like that."

"But she was under the pastor's control for an awfully long time." Jen sighed.

"I mean, those people did something their religion is against—murder!" cried Nique. "And they call it the Lord's work despite all the pain and suffering they caused. Gershwin helped a lot of those people in that church. Carl grew up in front of most of those people. Imagine if Gershwin hadn't sent Sara that video. Imagine how many more innocent people would've died because of their sick beliefs. If they don't put the blame on the devil, then they say it's the Lord's will. That's why people will never take responsibility—because they hide behind their Jesus and the devil."

"But Nique, you can't say things like that," whispered Jen. "People believe in what they believe in. And if they believe what they're doing is the right thing, never mind what is right or wrong, they're gonna follow their beliefs. Be grateful you know the difference between right and wrong. At the end of the day, each and every one of us will have to pay for our sins with death."

Nique pulled her bag onto her lap and searched for the pack of cigarettes that had sunk to the bottom.

"I just can't believe Pastor Richard did that to Gershwin," said Jen. "A pastor is supposed to be the leader in the community. It's funny how things happen. The morning those church followers wanted to bury Carl, they couldn't find the hole they had already dug for his body, so that's why they left him on the rugby field. I'm sure Pastor Richard didn't think he would end up like this.

He probably thought he wouldn't get caught."

Nique looked back up at Jen, cigarettes in her hand.

"That's what happens when you play God and when you have all that power over others," said Jen. "But I wish people would start thinking for themselves before they follow others blindly. I wish they wouldn't use their beliefs as an excuse to do horrible things to others."

"Pastor Richard was more than a pervert dressed up in a suit and tie with a Bible in his hand," Nique said. "He was such a coward to blame it all on Rose in the end."

"You're right about one thing, Nique," Jen said. "If it wasn't for Gershwin sending that video, then we wouldn't have known what happened, and that man wouldn't have come forward to tell us what was going on in that church. Gershwin probably didn't know it, but he caught the pigs that murdered Carl. He paid for it with his life."

"Yes, that's true," said Nique as Sara walked back into the bedroom.

"I'm scared another pastor like Richard will show up in the Shadows," Sara said. "We don't need people like that here."

"Gershwin died to bring some light into the Shadows," said Nique.

"He did," said Sara. "We need to make sure my unborn baby girl has a happier future here in the Shadows."

"Who says it's a girl, Sara?" asked Nique.

AUTHOR'S NOTE

The first edition of *Innie Shadows* was published in Kaaps. Kaaps is a language spoken by the Indigenous so-called Coloured, or mixed-race, people of South Africa, with different versions of Kaaps spoken throughout the country. Professor Adam Haupt, the director of the Centre for Film and Media Studies at the University of Cape Town, describes Kaaps as a language that was created in settler colonial South Africa and developed by the 1500s. The language took shape during encounters between Indigenous African (Khoi and San), Southeast Asian, Dutch, Portuguese, and English people. The Kaaps that we speak today, and that is found in *Innie Shadows*, is far from that early Kaaps that developed from the language created and spoken by the Indigenous and enslaved people of South Africa prior to the 1652 colonization period.

The history and context of the Kaaps language is just as layered as anything else that has been colonized. Kaaps was never previously recognized as a legitimate language.

The official language of South Africa was Afrikaans, and Kaaps was and is mostly known as a spoken dialect of Afrikaans. The Kaaps language movement is still very young. Only in 2021 was a project started to create a trilingual Kaaps dictionary, in Kaaps, English, and Afrikaans. This was a significant step forward for the Kaaps language movement so that Kaaps could be seen, read, and written in schools, universities, and other official spaces.

I was taught to read and write in Afrikaans and English. I first wrote the characters and the story that became *Innie Shadows* in English, but my master's thesis supervisor challenged me to rewrite the story in Kaaps, a language I had never written in before. It was in Kaaps that *Innie Shadows* was born. As I wrote in my home language, the title changed, the characters developed, and the story grew. I am proud to be one of the first authors to write a novel in Kaaps. I am ever grateful for this because it was and still is an honour to add to the growing literature of Kaaps.

ACKNOWLEDGEMENTS

Innie Shadows has been a ride that has taken me places I never thought I'd go. First I want to acknowledge *Innie Shadows* and its characters who invited me in to write and develop their story.

I want to acknowledge my publisher, Modjaji Books, who took a chance on a story written in a language that not many other publishers would publish. I want to thank and acknowledge House of Anansi Press and their editorial team and PEN Afrikaans for making this project possible. I also want to thank Words Without Borders, who first gave *Innie Shadows* a chance by publishing an English-translated excerpt on their platform in 2021. I am forever grateful for the support *Innie Shadows* has received.

I want to thank my wife and life partner for being on this adventure with me. I appreciate the love, support, and positive foundation you bring into my life. I want to thank and acknowledge my mom and my Ouma Anna. I am forever grateful for your love, guidance, and protection.

I want to thank and acknowledge all the people who've supported my work. Thank you.

Finally, I would like to acknowledge and honour all those who've lost their lives through prejudice, oppression, hatred, and homophobia. This world is less without you, but we look to a brighter future where homophobia, hatred, and oppression is something of the past. We will remember you.

And to you, the reader, I hope that you enjoyed meeting and engaging with the people of Shadow Heights as much as I did.

Thank you, sincerely yours, Olivia.

PHOTO BY A.C. & D.K

OLIVIA M. COETZEE was born in Mariental, a small town in southern Namibia. She found her voice and words in the township of Electric City, which is in Eerste Rivier, Cape Town. She is a passionate advocate for Kaaps being a written language as well as a spoken one. She has an MA in creative writing from the University of Cape Town.